LIGHT OF DAWN

BROKEN BOW

BOOK SIX

ASHLEY A QUINN

TCA PUBLISHING LLC

ISBN is 9781733160094
Library of Congress Control Number: 2021918389

ONE

"Stupid son-of-a..." Macy Brigg's voice trailed off as she tried to pop off the bottom plate on her espresso machine. She worked her flathead screwdriver between it and the machine's side, but it refused to budge. "Why won't you move?" She tipped her head to peer underneath. It had to be hung up on something.

"What are you doing?" Brady Archer's low voice cut through the sound of her tinkering.

Macy shrieked and straightened, turning to glare at him. "Jesus, Brady. Did you ghost through the door or something? I didn't hear you come in."

"It jingled." He hooked a thumb over his shoulder to point at the door with its bell.

She was sure it did. But she'd been absorbed in trying to fix her damn espresso machine. She set down her tools. "You want a coffee?"

He nodded. "What's wrong with it?" He pointed to the machine she was trying to fix.

"It sprung a leak. I'm trying to change out a fitting, but I can't get the bottom plate off to do it. I swear, I'm going to buy a new one. This one gives me nothing but problems." She poured him a large cup of black coffee as she spoke.

He frowned. "You want me to look at it?"

She waved a hand as she passed him the cup. "No, I'll figure it out. Just like every other time I've had to fix it."

His mouth turned down as he took the coffee. "You shouldn't have to keep fixing it. What's breaking?" He put the cup down on the counter and walked around to her side.

Macy stepped back as he invaded her space, her body going on red alert at his proximity. The man sent her hormones into overdrive with his gigantic frame, thick arms, and even thicker thighs. Then there was his face. With his square jaw, defined cheekbones, and dark beard, he could have just walked off the set of some biker drama. Brady Archer was sex personified.

He brushed past her, and Macy sighed. He didn't even know it. It was *maddening*.

"This the piece you're trying to take off?" He touched the chrome plate hanging crookedly from the bottom of the machine.

She nodded.

He bent nearly in half to peer at the underside. "You got a flashlight?"

"Yeah." She fished one from her toolbox and handed it to him.

He took off his hat and tossed it onto the display case, then clicked on the light, shining it up at the bottom. He picked up the screwdriver and dropped to his knees. Putting the small light between his teeth, he pushed up on the metal, looking for where it was hung up.

"Does this side panel come off?" he asked, taking the light out of his mouth.

"Only that bigger piece. You'd have to take apart a lot more of the frame to get that other piece off."

He grunted and fiddled with the plate, working the screwdriver between it and the frame. "It's caught on something."

"Duh."

He threw an annoyed glance at her, then went back to work. After a few more seconds of wiggling the screwdriver while supporting the plate, it popped free.

"Ha! Take that, you stupid machine!" Macy said.

Brady pulled the plate down and over the steam nozzles to look at it. "It's bent back here." He looked up at her. "What did you do to it?"

"I didn't do anything."

"It didn't bend itself, Mace."

"Maybe it bent the last time I had to take it off and put it back on. I don't know." She held out her hands, palms up. "I probably wasn't as gentle as I could have been. It was the third time I replaced the same part." She sighed. "This makes number four."

"That's not right. It shouldn't break that often." He looked at the machine, then back at her. "Show me where it's breaking. Maybe there's a different problem."

"If there is, I haven't been able to find it, even with help from the manufacturer's customer service and YouTube."

"Don't you have a warranty?"

"I do. But it doesn't cover replacement unless there's a catastrophic failure. The parts are covered, but I have to fix it, or find someone who can."

He frowned. "And after the fourth time you called for the same issue, they don't consider that catastrophic?"

"No. It still functions once the part is replaced. Trust me, it's cheaper for them to send me the new valves than to replace the entire machine."

"I bet. Okay. Show me where the problem is."

She leaned in to point at the valve he exposed, trying not to let the smell of him unnerve her. It was an intoxicating scent of leather, hay, and man. "That valve. Under that brass box is the fitting for the water pipe. The steamer nozzle comes off the front. It's leaking from the back. I replace the valve and it's fine for a couple months, then all of a sudden it's dripping a steady stream again."

Brady stared at the machine and scratched his head before picking up the wrench she'd laid out. He twisted off the fitting and removed the valve, shining the light in it. "I don't see any issue with the valve. It and the washer look fine." He turned his attention to the machine. "You said it's the rear of the valve that leaks?"

"Yep."

He leaned in closer, shining the light on the pipe he took the valve off of. "Have you replaced this pipe?"

"No." She leaned in. "Should I have?"

"I think so. Look at the threading on it." He pointed to the side. "See how it looks funny?"

"Yeah."

"It's rolled."

He turned to look at her at the same time she looked at him. Her eyes darted to his lips, which were inches away. She straightened, her face flaming, and cleared her throat. "How did that happen?"

"My guess is they over-tightened the valve when they put the machine together. You need a new water pipe if you ever want it to stop leaking."

Macy groaned. "I'll have to take the entire machine apart for that. That pipe winds through its innards."

"It won't be hard. Order the part, and I'll do it."

She wasn't sure she wanted to be indebted to him, but it would be nice not to have to take the machine apart and put it back together herself. She could do it, but it would take a million pictures, copious notes, and several hours. She could ask her brother, Declan, but he and Maggie just got married, and she hated to intrude on their evenings.

"You're sure? It'll take a couple hours, so it'll need to be in the evening."

He shrugged. "I'm sure. Feed me dinner and we'll call it square."

"Deal."

"Okay. Now, where's the new valve? Let's see if we can get this thing to work for now."

She handed him the part. "I need to take some pictures of the pipe threads to send to customer service before you put that on." She took out her phone and snapped a few pictures, then stepped back. "So, if it's the pipe, how come replacing the valve helps?"

"It's not so much the valve as it's the rubber washer in it. It gets compressed and loses some of its give the longer it's in there and the more you use the machine. Once that happens, because of the rolled threads, the valve gets loose and it leaks." He screwed on the new valve, then the steamer nozzle.

"Well, whatever the reason, I'm glad it won't leak for the foreseeable future. I'll call customer service and get the water pipe ordered today."

"Just let me know when it comes in, and I'll make time to come fix it." He reassembled the rest of the machine. Macy was a little perturbed that he did it in half the time it normally took her.

"Okay." She stepped back as he stood, looming tall over her. She spotted his coffee on the counter and picked it up to hand to him. "Thanks for fixing my machine. I appreciate it. Coffee's on me today."

He took the cup. "Thanks." He took a sip, watching her.

She tried not to squirm. Why did he always have to do that silent, brooding thing? It drove her nuts. He was a hard man to read, so she couldn't tell what he was thinking.

"I should get going." He picked up his hat and set it on his head, then turned and walked around the counter. "I need to get back to the ranch. Call me when that part comes in." He glanced back. "Or if it breaks again. I'll do what I can to keep it running."

Macy nodded. "Thanks, Brady."

He touched two fingers to his hat brim and pushed through the door. The bell jingled as he exited at the same time the kitchen door opened behind her. She glanced back and smiled as she saw Denise James come through.

"Was that Brady?"

"Yeah. He stopped in for coffee and fixed the espresso machine. For now, anyway. He found a bigger problem with it."

She frowned. "Is it okay to use?"

"It's fine. The threading on the pipe going into the valve is rolled, so it doesn't line up right. The new valve will hold it at bay for a bit until the washer ages some."

"Oh. All right." She walked closer, tying her apron on.

"Kids get off to school okay?"

"Yes. They were quite eager to start their day. You and Declan telling them you're taking them camping in a couple weeks lit a fire under them. They don't dilly dally anymore. They want the days to pass quickly, so it's time for that trip."

Macy smiled. "I want that too. Declan and I are looking forward to it." They'd been planning this trip for a couple months. Ever since Denise and the girls moved to Silver Gap. The first thing Jessie asked—after whether she could ride a horse—was when they could go camping. Hannah echoed it, and the next thing Macy knew, she and Declan were planning a camping trip.

But she didn't mind. She was eager to spend time with them. Getting to know her younger sisters was amazing. After everything that happened in November, she was grateful for the opportunity. And her blossoming friendship with the girls' mother was a wonderful bonus. Denise was proving to be a hard worker and a good friend. It was great to see her thriving in her new surroundings.

The bell over the door dinged, admitting several people, and shaking Macy from her thoughts.

"Looks like the rush is on its way."

"Yep. I'm going to go email the pictures I took of the pipe to customer service before we get slammed. I'll be right back."

Denise nodded, stepping toward the register to greet their customers. "I got this. Go."

Macy smiled and scampered through the kitchen door to where it was quiet. She jotted a quick email to her customer service rep and uploaded the pictures, then hit send. Noise from the café increased, and she frowned. What was going on?

She stepped through the door to see the district attorney, Daniel Kerr, frowning at Denise, coffee soaking his front.

"Oh my goodness. What happened?" Macy rushed forward, grabbing a towel and handing it to him.

He dabbed at the liquid staining his clothes. "My coffee spilled."

Denise looked at Macy with watery eyes. "I'm so sorry. I went to hand him back his card and my hand hit the cup."

She touched the other woman on the shoulder. "It was an accident. I'm sure Mr. Kerr understands." Macy glanced at the D.A., daring him to contradict her.

He returned her stare as he swiped at his clothes. "Yes. An accident."

"See?" Macy said. "No harm done except to his clothes. But he lives close, so I'm sure he'll be able to run home and change." She spun around and grabbed a large empty cup, filling it full of the house brew coffee Kerr liked. She snapped a lid on it and held it out to him. "I know you already paid, so next one is on the house."

He traded her the towel for the coffee. "Thank you." With a nod, he turned and left.

Denise's shoulders dropped, and she looked up at Macy. "I can't believe I did that. I feel terrible. I hope it didn't hurt too much. He kept frowning so hard."

Macy rolled her eyes. "He wasn't in pain. He's just a grumpy bastard."

That surprised a laugh from Denise.

Macy smiled. "It's true. I don't think he's a very happy man."

"Well, regardless, I still feel terrible." She bit her lip. "Do you think he'd appreciate it if I made him a pie?"

Macy's eyebrows shot up. "You want to bake Daniel Kerr a pie?"

Denise frowned. "Is that bad?"

"No. I just can't see him eating pie. Not because I don't think yours would be good," she rushed to assure Denise, "but because he's got a stick up his ass that's lodged tight." Macy didn't have a high opinion of the man. He struck her as a jerk even before he tried to railroad her brother for murder and kidnapping. He was lucky she let him walk through the door.

"Really?" Denise glanced at the door. "He doesn't seem that way to me. He's always been polite. A little reserved maybe, but not rude."

"Why, Denise, do you have a crush on the D.A.?" Macy grinned.

Denise blushed. "I'll admit, he's not bad to look at, but he'd never be interested in a woman like me."

"Don't sell yourself short. You've really turned your life around. And you're a good person. So you made a bad decision years and years ago to get involved with my dad. He's out of your life now. And you have the benefit of never having been arrested, despite your involvement with him. Any man would be proud to be with a strong woman like you. Kerr's just a stuffed suit who wouldn't know a good thing if it bit him on the ass. Someone better will come along. You'll see."

Denise laughed. "I love your optimism, Macy."

"Choosing to be happy is all we have."

"Hmm." Denise arched a brow at her. "Are you doing that? Because I think if you wanted to be truly happy, Brady wouldn't have walked out that door without a kiss."

Macy's face turned red.

"I don't know what you're waiting for," Denise continued. "You two are obviously attracted to each other." She shook her head. "I'm not taking any relationship advice from you until you follow your own."

"Then you're doomed to wait. Brady Archer isn't interested in me. And I have no desire to embarrass myself in front of him."

Denise patted her shoulder. "You keep telling yourself that. I've seen the way he looks at you. You're as blind as he is." She turned away to help the next customer, leaving Macy to contemplate her words.

Did Brady have feelings for her? She'd certainly never seen any indication of that. The man needed to go to Vegas and enter a poker tournament. His face gave away nothing.

The bell over the door tinkled again, admitting several more people. Macy shrugged off her thoughts. They would have to wait. Right now, the morning rush was upon them and required her full attention.

With Denise by her side as well as two other young women she employed, Macy slogged through the rush. Tara waddled through the door near the end of it.

"What are you doing here? You're supposed to be taking it easy." Tara's due date was only two weeks away, and her doctor told her to rest as much as possible in an attempt to control some of the swelling she experienced now that the end of her pregnancy was near.

"I have been. But I can only stare at the walls of my living room so much before I go a little stir-crazy. A trip to town to talk to you and get a decaf latte won't hurt anything. I'll go right back to the couch when I get home."

Macy grinned and punched the button on her coffee grinder to grind up some decaf espresso beans. "Sure you will. On your way past London's, no doubt."

Tara lifted a shoulder, a smile tugging at one corner of her mouth. "She might have mentioned the other day that she was making cinnamon rolls for breakfast today."

Macy's mouth watered. "Lucky. I'm stuck here and can't go get one."

"She might bring some over after her guests eat if you ask nicely." Tara started to smile, then put a hand on her back and grimaced.

"You okay?" Macy paused in pouring the milk into the latte as she took in her friend's expression.

Tara rubbed the small of her back. "Yeah. I've just had a backache the last day or so. It's getting worse. My body is done carrying Jace's giant spawn."

Macy giggled. "Have you seen your brothers? Not all of their size comes from your husband."

Tara grimaced again before she could reply. She held her back with one hand and handed Denise her credit card with the other.

"This back pain—is it coming in waves?" Denise asked. "Or does it just get worse with movement?"

"Waves."

Denise grinned. "Well, I don't think you'll have to carry his spawn much longer. I think you're in labor."

Tara's eyes grew large. "What? No. I can't be. This doesn't feel anything like labor pains. The ones I had with Lucy were excruciating."

"Every pregnancy is different. And you're carrying twins.

To term."

"Are you sure?" Macy asked.

Denise nodded. "I had back pain with Hannah before the contractions started. I thought it was just from carrying the extra weight, too, until I went in for my doctor's appointment and the doctor told me I was in labor."

Macy popped a lid on the latte and hurried around the counter. She took Tara by the elbow and led her to a table. "You should sit. And we need to call Jace."

"No!" Tara sank into a chair and took the latte from Macy's hand. "He will freak if you call him and tell him I'm in labor without a plan of action. Let me call my doctor first and see what she says. *Then*, I'll call Jace." She set the coffee down and opened her purse to take out her phone. "Oh!" At her surprised cry, she hunched forward.

"What?" Macy crouched in front of her. "What's wrong?"

Tara looked up, shock etched on her face. "My water broke."

Macy glanced down to see a small puddle forming on the floor and more fluid dripping off the chair. "Crap!" She rose. "Okay. We need to get you to the hospital."

"Go," Denise said. "The girls and I will hold down the fort."

"Okay, good. Thank you." Macy inhaled a deep breath through her nose, trying to steady her rioting emotions. "Can you get me a few bar towels to protect the car seat?"

Denise nodded and hurried away. Macy took Tara by the forearms and helped her stand. "Can you walk?"

Hunched, Tara nodded. "So long as we go slow. Damn. It feels like there's a boulder between my hips now."

"Well, they're not floating anymore, so I'm not surprised. Just hold on to me and we'll get you to the car." She wrapped an arm around Tara's waist and clutched her hand. Denise followed them to the door with the towels, holding it open.

Just over the threshold, Tara stopped, groaning. Her grip on Macy's hand tightened, her knuckles turning white. "Oh, God!"

Macy glanced at Denise. "Find her keys."

Denise slid Tara's purse off her arm and opened it, rooting through the contents to find the key ring.

Tara blew out a breath and straightened as much as she was able. "Okay. It passed. Let's go before another one hits."

As fast as they were able, they moved down the sidewalk to Tara's SUV. Denise unlocked it and opened the passenger door, spreading the towels over the seat. Macy helped her friend inside, then took Tara's purse and keys from Denise, running around the hood to jump in the driver's seat. "I'll call you later," she told the other woman.

"You better. We'll all want an update."

Macy nodded and shut the door. She started the engine and put the car in reverse, backing onto the street. "You doing okay?" She glanced over at her friend.

Tara nodded, rubbing her hands over her distended abdomen. "Yeah. A little in shock, but I'm okay. I guess I should call Jace now."

Macy chuckled and made the turn onto the road that ran in front of the hospital. "Probably wouldn't be a bad idea. I could just swing into the police station and pick him up."

Tara giggled. "That would be a sight." She took her phone from her purse. "Seeing as I'm leaking all over the front seat, I'll just call him before I do irreparable damage to the uphol-stery." She touched a couple icons on her phone, then put it to her ear.

"Hey, babe. So, I went to town to get a coffee and went into labor in Peppy Brewster."

Macy could hear his shout of surprise come through loud and clear.

"I'm fine. Macy's driving me to the hospital now. In fact, we just pulled in." She paused to listen.

Macy pulled up to the portico at the emergency department.

"Okay. See you in a minute." She hung up and looked at Macy. "He's on his way."

"Good." She put the car in park. "I'm going to get you a wheelchair."

Tara groaned. "I'm not an invalid."

"No, but Jace will kill me if I make you walk."

Tara tried to smile, but her face soured and she sucked in a breath as another contraction took hold. Macy jumped out of the car. Time to move. She dashed through the ER doors. The girl at the desk looked up.

"I've got Tara Travers outside. She's in labor." Macy headed for a cluster of wheelchairs, grabbing one.

"I'll page obstetrics," the woman said.

Macy wheeled the chair outside and helped Tara out of the car. She fell into the chair with a groan. "Ugh. I'm already ready for this to be over."

"It will be soon." Macy patted her on the shoulder. "Then you'll have two beautiful babies to love on."

Tara was silent. Macy glanced down to see a tear roll down her friend's cheek. She stopped the chair. "Hey. What's wrong?"

"Nothing." Tara waved a hand. "It just hit me. In a few hours, I'll be a mom. There will be two babies in my house. I can hardly believe it. The last time I was in this position, I knew things wouldn't turn out that way."

Macy bent down and wrapped her arms around Tara's shoulders to give her a hug. "I'm so happy for you, T. You deserve this. You're going to be the best mom."

Tara patted her arm and sniffed. "Thank you. Now, wheel me inside so I can get them out of me."

Macy laughed and straightened. She pushed the chair toward the doors, which swished open to admit them. As they crossed the threshold, she heard boots pounding on the pavement and turned to see Jace running toward them at full speed. He flew through the door and skidded to a stop.

"Are you okay?" He dropped to his knees next to his wife.

"I'm fine. According to Denise, though, my backache was early labor. My water broke at the coffee shop and now I'm having contractions."

"Well, shit."

She reached out to touch his cheek. "Are you ready for this? We're going to be parents again."

He laid his hand over hers. "I'm so ready. I can't wait to meet our babies."

Macy fanned her face as tears threatened. "You two are going to make me cry."

Jace smiled and stood up. "God forbid." He glanced around. "Let's get this show on the road." He took over the handlebars on the wheelchair and steered Tara toward the registration desk.

The woman smiled. "I already called obstetrics. Someone should be down shortly to get you."

"Thank you," Tara said. Jace turned her around and pushed her over to a bank of chairs to wait.

"I'm going to run to your house and get your hospital bag," Macy said.

"It's in the master bedroom closet," Tara said.

"Is there anything else you want me to grab?"

"No. Everything is in that bag."

"Okay. I'll be back soon."

"Thanks, Macy," Jace said.

"Any time." She gave Tara's hand a squeeze, then retreated outside. Excitement strummed through her, quickening her pace. It was baby time.

Two

Brady paced in the hospital waiting room, pausing to stare out the third-floor window at the parking lot below. How long did it take to have a baby? Nerves sent him back across the floor, and his eyes strayed to the door leading to the maternity ward. Tara had been in labor for over nine hours now, and according to Macy, she'd unknowingly been in early labor for a couple of days before that. It had to be soon.

"Brady, honey, maybe you should wander downstairs and get a cup of coffee," Jenny said from her seat by the door. "Just make sure it's decaf."

He stopped to look at his mother. "Sorry, I'm just worried." The last time his sister gave birth, things hadn't turned out so well.

"She's fine. Someone would have come out if there was anything wrong."

He sat down in an empty chair next to Declan and crossed his ankle over his knee. His foot bobbed for several seconds before he stood up again and wandered back to the window. The elevator dinged, making him turn. His muscles grew tense for another reason as Macy emerged. A bolt of pure lust punched him in the gut at the sight of her. She was still in her jeans and Peppy Brewster tee, but she'd thrown a gray cardigan over it under her winter coat. Her dark auburn hair was tucked into a messy bun on top of her head with a pencil. Brady wanted to pull that pencil out and watch the rusty tresses cascade down her shoulders so he could run his fingers through them. He stuffed his hands in his pockets and looked out the window again.

Why did Macy have to tie him up in knots? Why did any woman, for that matter? He liked his solitude. When the urge for companionships struck, he knew several bars in Pueblo where he could always find a willing woman for the night. He didn't need or want a relationship. But his body didn't care. It wanted Macy, and it was getting harder all the time to keep his hands to himself.

The door across the room opened, and Brady turned. Jace stepped out, smiling from ear to ear.

"It's a boy and a girl. Mom and babies are doing great."

Relief made Brady's shoulders sag, and he stepped forward with the rest of his family to congratulate him.

"When can we see them?" Jenny asked.

"Soon. They're getting them cleaned up and doing their assessments." He took his phone from his pocket. "I took some pictures." Everyone crowded around, oohing and ahhing over the two dark-haired babies swaddled up to their chubby chins.

"Good lord, they're chunky," Seb said.

"Not too much, really," Jace said. "It's the way they have them wrapped. They both weigh just over seven pounds."

"These kids have names?" Thomas asked. "Or haven't you decided yet? You were bandying several around."

"They do. We wanted to honor their sisters, so we used their first initials. Hudson Lane, and Lydia Hazel."

Emotion tugged at Brady's heart as he thought of the

nieces he'd never met. A glance around at the others revealed they were all fighting tears, some losing the battle, Macy included.

Jace pocketed his phone. "I better get back. Once they say you can come visit, I'll come back out."

"Give her our love," Jenny said.

"I will."

"Congratulations, son." Lee held out his hand.

Jace took it, a wide grin on his face. "Thank you. I'll be back as soon as I can." He spun around, waving his bracelet over the reader next to the door, then pushed through.

"I don't know about the rest of you, but I'm going to go eat," Lee announced. He held out an arm to his wife. "Join me for cafeteria pizza, my love?"

Jenny giggled and looped her arm through his. "I'd love to."

Lee smiled down at her, then looked up at the rest of them. "Any of the rest of you want to join us?"

A chorus of yeses filled the room.

"Those poor cafeteria workers aren't going to know what hit them," Macy said, following the eldest Archers to the elevator.

Lee gave his children the stink eye as he got on the elevator. "She's right. You all need to be on your best behavior."

"We aren't toddlers, Dad," Maggie said.

"No, but you're still loud." He shook a finger at her, but looked at them all. "Inside voices." The elevator doors closed with all but Brady, Macy, Declan, and Maggie inside.

"I'm going to take the stairs," Brady said. There was no point waiting for the elevator when there was an alternative.

"Sounds good to me." Macy jogged ahead of him to the door, but he reached around her, pulling it open. Maggie and Declan stepped through. Macy followed, with Brady right behind her.

Her bun bobbed, slipping as she walked down the steps. She reached up with one slender arm and pulled the pencil free. Brady had to put a hand on the railing as it cascaded down in rich, coppery waves. He bit back a groan. Maybe dinner with the family wasn't such a great idea.

They pushed through the stairwell door to see the rest of the family waiting. Together, they meandered down the corridor to the cafeteria. Brady kept his distance from Macy as they walked, knowing if he didn't, the temptation to touch all her glorious hair would be too strong to resist. His emotions were running at a high because of Tara, so his defenses were lower than usual.

Turning into the cafeteria, Brady headed for the sandwich line to get a hot sub. Once he had his food in hand, he found a seat at the end of the long table his family commandeered, thanking his lucky stars when Thomas sat next to him. He could still hear Macy laughing with his sisters-in-law, but at least he wasn't sitting right next to her, feeling her presence within reach.

As they finished their meals, Lee's phone dinged with a text from Jace to let them know they could come back and visit. Brady dumped his trash and followed his parents out of the cafeteria.

Back upstairs, he settled into a chair, chatting with Declan while they waited for their turn to go back. The nurses wouldn't let them all back at once, so they went in groups of four, with his parents and Seb and London going first. Declan, Maggie, Thomas, and Rayna would go next, leaving him and Macy to go last. By the time it was their turn, he was edgy from listening to her talk and laugh with the others, her voice driving a steady throb of desire straight to his groin.

Teeth clenched and trying to tamp down his simmering arousal, he followed her down the hallway to Tara's room. She rapped her knuckles on the door and peeked around the edge.

Brady kept his eyes off her silky, fragrant hair and tried to look around her into the room.

"Hello?" She pushed the door open

"Hi." Tara's quiet voice floated to them.

Brady walked in behind Macy and saw his sister sitting up in bed, holding a wrapped bundle. Jace sat next to her in a chair, holding another.

Macy squealed and stepped forward. "Gimme. I don't care which one."

Jace and Tara laughed.

"Here." Tara lifted the baby in her arms. "Take Lydia."

"Gladly." Macy took the baby with the bow hat on her head and tucked her close. "Ooo! I could eat her up. She's adorable."

"She's not a cookie, Mace," Brady said. His voice was a little gruffer than he intended. Seeing Macy holding a baby did something to him he didn't want to acknowledge.

She looked at him with a frown. "Take that baby from Jace and tell me you don't want to love all over him."

Jace stood and put Hudson in his arms. Brady looked down at the tiny human squirming in the confines of his blanket. An instant wash of love spread through him as he took in his nephew's face. He stroked the baby's soft cheek with one finger. "Hi, buddy. I'm your Uncle Brady. I'm the best one of your uncles. Thomas will try to tell you it's him because he's your mom's twin, but don't listen to him. He's full of horsesh —crap."

Macy snorted. "Horse crap isn't much better."

"Is too." He kept his voice soft. "Don't listen to her, either."

"Turning him against me already?" She sidled closer, leaning in to get a better look at Hudson's face. Her hair slid over his forearm, sending an electric jolt straight through him to his crotch. *Jesus. What the hell was wrong with him?* It had apparently been far too long since he was with a woman if he couldn't keep his mind off sex at a time like this.

Macy looked up at him, a smile on her pretty face. Her indigo eyes shone bright in the harsh overhead lights.

Or maybe it was just Macy.

Brady cleared his throat and shifted, using the guise of adjusting the baby in his arms to a different position to step away from her enticing presence.

"They're a good mix of both of you," Macy said.

"Except for the hair," Jace said. "I think I'm destined to have dark-haired kids now."

Brady grinned. "Yeah. The Archer genes are strong. Poor Mom never stood a chance, and neither did you." He glanced at Macy. It was a shame. He wouldn't mind a baby with her blue eyes.

Holy fuck! Where did that thought come from? He looked down at Hudson, attempting to keep his thoughts off his face.

"Trade me," Macy said.

"What?" He glanced up.

"Trade me. I want to hold him."

"Oh. Right." He shifted the baby, putting him in her other arm, then taking Lydia. As he did with her brother, he touched her cheek and introduced himself. She turned her head, her tiny mouth open as she searched for his finger. One miniscule fist popped free of the blanket to wave in the air. He grabbed it between his thumb and forefinger. She latched on with a grip much stronger than he expected. Love welled in his chest for this little girl who had the same fighting spirit as her mother.

He looked up at his sister, who rested against the pillows with a soft, happy smile on her tired face. "You did good, T. They're beautiful."

Her smile grew radiant. "Thank you."

They chatted a while longer until Lydia let out a mewling

cry. Her open mouth rubbed against his knuckle. "I think this one's hungry." He stepped to the bed and handed the baby back to Tara.

"Probably." She glanced at the clock. "I didn't realize so much time had passed since you all started visiting."

"It's getting late, anyway," Macy said. She handed Hudson to Jace. "We'll head out and let you feed them and get some rest. Let us know if you need anything."

"We will," Jace said.

"Thanks for everything you did today, Macy."

"All I did was drive. And not even that far."

"Still. It's appreciated."

"You're welcome. We'll see you later."

Brady echoed her farewell with a wave.

"Goodnight," Tara said. Jace smiled.

They stepped out into the hall and made their way down the corridor to enter the waiting room. Brady frowned when he took in the empty space.

"Where did they all go?"

"Probably home. It's been a long day."

"Yeah, but Mom and Dad were my ride."

"You didn't drive yourself?"

He shook his head. "No. We finished the ranch chores, then drove in together. It didn't make sense to take two cars."

Macy sighed and ran a hand through her loose hair. "Come on. I'll drive you home."

Brady's defenses went up as the light, summery fragrance of her hair assaulted his senses. "You don't have to do that. I'll call Dad or Thomas and make them come get me since they stranded me here."

"Now what doesn't make sense? Why should they drive all the way back to town, then home again when I'm already here?"

"But then you have to drive back. That's not any better. It's still a full trip."

She waved a hand and picked up their coats, handing him his. "Let them rest. Besides, they're all probably fielding a million questions from the kids." She took a fistful of the front of his shirt and tugged, heading for the elevator. "Let's go."

He sucked in a breath at the feel of her fingers on his abdomen through the fabric of his shirt. It sent a bolt of need straight through him. He was thankful when she let go to push the call button.

The elevator dinged and the doors slid open. She stepped inside and turned, arching a brow when he stood there and stared at her. "Coming?"

Blood rushed south, making his jeans uncomfortable. Oh, if she only knew. The doors started to close, but she shot a hand out to hold them open.

"Get on the elevator, Brady."

He steeled himself and stepped inside.

"What is your problem?"

"Nothing. I'm just tired. It's been a long day." He prayed she wouldn't call bullshit. He frequently put in longer days on the ranch than this.

"It has been a bit of an emotional rollercoaster, that's for sure." The doors slid closed, and the car descended. The ride was quick, letting them out in the lobby moments later. He shrugged into his coat and followed her outside to her car. Inside, she adjusted the heat, then put the car in gear and headed out of town toward his family's ranch. Brady rested his head against the seat and tried not to think about the woman sitting next to him.

"I ordered that part," she said a few minutes into their drive. "It's supposed to be here Monday. They put a rush on it."

"Okay. I'll come into town Monday evening and get it changed out." He rolled his head against the seat to look at her. "What are you making me for dinner?" A smile quirked a corner of his mouth.

She chuckled. "What do you want?"

He thought for a minute about things she'd made in the past. "Chili? You make good chili."

"I can do chili. That actually works really well. I can throw it in the slow cooker in the morning and it'll be ready by dinnertime."

"And cornbread?"

"Who eats chili without cornbread?"

"Weird people."

"Very weird." She laughed. "Thank you again for offering to fix the machine. It would have taken me hours and several days of how-to videos to do it myself."

"Not a problem. I'm just glad I can fix it."

"Me too. I'm tired of changing valves."

He chuckled and looked out the windshield again. Dark shapes whizzed by as she drove down the road past the national forest land. The sky hung low, blotting out any moonlight. It was going to snow again.

Even as the thought hit him, snowflakes drifted down, highlighted by the car's headlights. In the distance, he could see the pole light on the ranch driveway. Macy slowed when she reached it and turned down the lane. She bumped down the stone drive, which was full of potholes now that the weather was more up and down, and stopped at the gate to enter the code that would let them through to the family compound. The high metal structure rolled open, and she drove through. It closed behind them.

She made the turn into his driveway and shifted the car into park.

"Thanks for the ride." The interior light came on as he

opened his door. "Be careful driving back, please. The roads might be a little slick." The snow was picking up.

"I will. I'll see you Monday."

He nodded. "Goodnight."

"Goodnight."

Brady closed the door and headed for his front door, unlocking it and slipping inside as she pulled away. He let out a breath, closing his eyes for a brief moment, some of the tension leaving him now that he was away from her. He had to do something about the way she made him feel. Finding a willing woman in one of the larger towns or taking care of himself in the shower wasn't cutting it anymore.

He just needed a break from her. In the last few months, she'd been around a lot more because of Declan and Maggie's wedding. After he fixed her espresso machine on Monday, he needed to distance himself from her. Getting involved with Macy Briggs—or any woman—wasn't on his to-do list.

Three

The bell over the door tinkled. Macy looked back from cleaning the machines, expecting to see Brady. She straightened when she saw it was someone else.

"Mr. Kerr. It's a bit late for coffee for you. Or are you working late tonight?"

He walked closer. Even after a full day in the office, his suit still looked impeccable, but the tired lines on his face gave away his long day.

"I work late many evenings, but that's not why I'm here. Is Ms. James around?"

"You want to talk to Denise?" She narrowed her eyes at him. "Is this about the coffee thing from last week? Because I'll tell you now, if you intend to slap some lawsuit on her for—"

He waved a hand, cutting her off. "It's not about that." He paused and frowned. "Well, it is. Sort of. But there's no lawsuit." He sighed. "Despite what you think of me, I'm not a bad guy. Overly ambitious at times, but not bad. Now, is she here?"

Macy eyed him for another moment before nodding. "She's in the back, putting away inventory." She stepped to the kitchen door and poked her head through, asking the other woman to come out front. The door swung closed as Macy turned around. "She'll be out in a second."

He nodded.

She went back to cleaning, but picked the display case so she could keep an eye on him. The door swung out and Denise stepped through. She saw Kerr and smiled.

"Mr. Kerr, hello. Did you get the pie I left with your assistant?"

"That's why I'm here, yes." He brushed a lock of his salt and pepper hair from his forehead. "I wanted to thank you in person for bringing it by. It was a pleasant surprise. Apple's my favorite and yours was some of the best I've ever had."

Denise beamed. "Really? That's wonderful. I'm so glad you liked it. I really am sorry for dumping coffee on you."

He smiled, and Denise blushed. Macy stood to the side in a bit of shock. What was going on?

"If it gets me more pie, you can dump coffee on me whenever you want."

"When's your birthday? I'll bring you one then."

"Not until October."

Her face pulled down in a frown. "Well, perhaps for Easter, then. That's only a month away."

"I'd like that." His eyes darted past her and he rolled his bottom lip in before releasing it. "Um, I know it's short notice, but would you like to grab a bite to eat with me tonight? Your daughters are welcome to come too. We could go to Boone's."

Denise blinked at him. Macy leaned against the display. This was better than any soap opera.

"You realize who I am, right?" Denise said. "Mistress and mother of the men arrested for arson and murder?"

He nodded. "I do. But I also know you're not them. We all make mistakes. And you're also the nicest, sweetest woman

I've met in a long time. I could use a dose of sweetness in my life, to be honest." A furrow formed between his brows. "I've spent too many years with the dregs of society and it's made me bitter. You're like a breath of fresh air."

Who was this man, and what did he do with the real Daniel Kerr? "Did you hit your head?" Macy couldn't stop the words from popping free. She waved her hands. "Sorry, that was rude. But seriously, what the hell?"

"What she said," Denise added.

"No, I did not hit my head. No, I haven't lost my mind. I just—" he broke off and started again. "I want a change."

"And you think I'm the change you need?" She shared a look with Macy. "Honey, I'm not interested in being your mid-life crisis."

"It's not that, either. Just, please consider having dinner with me? It doesn't have to be tonight."

Macy held her breath as Denise studied him.

"I'll think about it."

A hopeful light bloomed in his eyes and he smiled. "Thank you. I should go and let you two finish closing up. Have a good evening." With a wave, he turned and strode toward the door. Brady stepped through the door as he reached it. Kerr offered him a nod, then stepped through.

"Lock that," Macy said.

Brady turned the lock and flipped the sign to closed, glancing through the glass at Kerr's retreating form before turning his attention to them. "What was he doing here this time of day?"

"He asked me out."

His eyebrows shot up as he looked at Denise. "Daniel Kerr asked you out?"

Denise nodded. "I know. Color me surprised too."

"What did you say?"

"That I'd think about it. What do you know about him?"

Brady shrugged. "Not too much. He's a local. His dad was the D.A. at one point, then a judge. His mom died of cancer when he was young. He's had a succession of stepmothers since. Judge Kerr retired about ten years ago. He and his wife moved to southern California after that. Dan's got a sister, too, somewhere. I think she's an attorney in one of the big cities. New York, Chicago, some place like that. You'd have to ask Maggie. She knows more."

"Is he a good guy?"

"He's not awful. I mean, Seb cleaned house at the courthouse, and he survived the cull. So, he's either really good at hiding it, or not a corrupt asshole."

Denise frowned, a thoughtful look on her face.

"Whatever you decide, you have our support," Macy said. "If you go out with him and he turns out to be a jerk, he'll have to suffer the Archer wrath. Plus, find a new place to get his morning coffee." She grinned. She would gladly lose a customer if it kept Denise happy.

Denise giggled. "That's good to know. I'll think about it." She stepped back toward the kitchen door. "I'm going to finish the last couple boxes, then head home."

"Sounds good. See you tomorrow." Macy smiled at her, and she disappeared through the door.

Brady leaned on the counter, watching as she went back to cleaning. "Why are you cleaning? I'm going to make a mess."

"I'm just wiping up all the sticky stuff. It's easier to wipe it off one surface than to clean it off all the machine parts."

"I guess that's true."

She glanced at him, noting the tired lines around his dark eyes. His mouth drooped behind his beard. "You okay?"

"I'm fine. Just a rough day. We had a couple cows calve and they were tough births. We lost one of the calves. And I'm not a hundred percent certain we won't lose the mom, too."

"I'm sorry."

He shrugged. "That's ranch life. I'm just tired."

"I can brew a pot of coffee, if you want."

"Actually, if you wouldn't mind, that would be great."

"Sure." She turned away, but not before she got a view of that muscled chest, pushing the seams of his shirt as he took off his coat.

"Where's the part for the machine? I'll get started."

"It's in my office." She took a key ring from her pocket and handed it to him. "The toolbox is in there too."

He took the keys. "I'll be right back." He walked around the counter to go through the kitchen door.

Macy did her best to focus on making coffee, but she couldn't help herself and glanced up as he walked away. Brady's butt in a pair of jeans was probably the best thing she'd ever laid eyes on. He really should be the star of a commercial for blue jeans. If they put his ass on an ad graphic, women everywhere would buy those pants for their men.

She shook her head at her thoughts. She had it bad.

Brady wiped his wet hands and reached for his coffee cup, taking a sip before picking up the new pipe for the espresso machine. He had the old one out. Now he just needed to reassemble everything with the new pipe in place.

The kitchen door swung open and Macy stepped through, bringing some delicious smells with her.

"The chili's done. The cornbread will be by the time you finish putting that thing back together. I made chocolate chip cookies for dessert too. I used London's recipe."

Brady's mouth watered. He'd been looking forward to this meal all day. The cookies were a bonus. "Okay. Can you come here and hold this?"

She stepped up beside him, putting her coppery waves

right under his nose. He did his best to block out the scent of her hair and concentrate.

"Right here?" She put her hand next to his on the pipe.

"No. On the outside of that housing. There's only room to put one hand inside and still be able to tighten the nut."

She moved her hand, and he slid his up to find the end of the pipe. He lined the piece up with the valve on the other end and spun the nut, tightening it until he couldn't turn it with his fingers. "You can let go." He picked up a wrench and slipped it around the nut to tighten it further.

"You know where the rest of this goes, right?"

He looked at her to see her eyeing the array of parts on the counter. "Relax, Mace. I know what I'm doing."

"You've fixed an espresso machine before?"

"Yes."

Her eyes shot to his. "When?"

"The other day, when I put that valve on for you."

She laughed, making him smile.

"Okay, I deserved that. But seriously, you remember where all of this goes?"

He nodded. "Machines just make sense to me." He picked up another part and the screws to reattach it. "I'll have this done by the time that cornbread comes out of the oven."

"If you say so. I'm going to go set a table for us. Unless you need my help still?"

Brady glanced over the parts he had to put back together. "No. I think that was the only tricky part." Truthfully, he would be glad to have her off doing something else. Her presence was distracting.

"Okay, then." She pushed away from the counter and walked away.

He turned his attention to the machine, reassembling it with deft hands. By the time she had the table set, complete with food, he was done.

"You didn't beat the cornbread," she said, setting the last bowl on the table.

A corner of his mouth lifted, and he shrugged. "I was close. I'm going to go wash my hands quick and put these tools away."

"I'll help."

Before he could protest that he could get it, she was next to him, putting tools back in the toolbox. When she reached in front of him to grab the last wrench, he had to hold his breath and take a step back. She smelled like flowers and chocolate. He suddenly wanted more than the chili and cornbread waiting for him.

He cleared his throat. "Why don't you put that back in your office while I wash up?"

She nodded. He hurried through the kitchen door to the bathroom. As he soaped his hands, he stared at his reflection in the mirror. He was a damn fool for asking for dinner in return for fixing the espresso machine. He shouldn't have asked for anything. Just fixed the fucker and run. Now he was stuck sitting at a table with her while they ate. Alone.

He shut the water off and dried his hands, having lingered as long as he could, then made his way back to the front of the café. Macy sat at the table, scrolling through her phone. She looked up as he walked in.

"You ready to eat?" She put the phone down and picked up a bowl.

"Yes." He sat down across from her.

She ladled chili into the bowl and handed it to him. He picked up the bag of shredded cheese and poured some on top. She passed him a thick slice of cornbread on a plate before adding soup to her own bowl.

"Thanks." He picked up his knife and took some of the butter on the table, slathering it on his cornbread.

She smiled at him. "You're welcome."

Brady dipped his spoon in his chili and kept his head down as he ate. He just wanted to finish and go home before he opened his mouth and said something dumb. Macy tongue-tied him regularly when there were people around. He could only imagine what she would do now that there was no one else here to carry the conversation.

"Read any good books lately?"

He paused, the spoon inches from his mouth, and glanced at her. "Huh?" *Brilliant, Brady. Just brilliant.* He sounded like a damn caveman.

"Books. I know you read a lot. Did you read any good ones lately?"

"Um," he cleared his throat. "Yeah, a few." He shoved the spoon in his mouth.

"Such as?" She took a bite of her cornbread.

"Some war books. I've been on a bronze age war kick lately."

"Were they fiction?"

"Mostly. I read a couple non-fiction ones, which got me wondering about fiction set in that era."

"We're talking Stonehenge era, right?"

He nodded.

"Cool. I'd love to go there. And the pyramids. They're engineering marvels. It's so interesting to think that people built such structures without modern tools."

"Man can do a lot with just his hands and his brain." He dipped his bread in the chili and took a bite.

"You certainly can. I'm going to start calling you MacGyver."

"I didn't do any MacGyvering to your espresso machine. I just replaced a part."

"Right, but you've done plenty with other things."

Brady shrugged, feeling slightly embarrassed. He hated

when people paid him a compliment. He never knew how to respond.

Silence fell. He concentrated on the remainder of his meal. Or tried to, anyway. He could feel her eyes on him. He refused to look at her until he finished, though. Those blue eyes would turn him into a stuttering fool.

"Brady, can I ask you something?"

He nodded, still staring at his food.

"Why don't you date?"

The hunk of cornbread he just swallowed lodged in his throat. He picked up his water glass and took several hearty swallows before looking at her.

"That's rather personal."

She shrugged and stared at him. Brady felt his cheeks heat. *Dammit.* Why did he always get so flustered around this woman?

"Why the interest in my dating life?"

"I was thinking about Denise and Dan, which led me to think about all the new relationships around us lately. We're the odd ones out. So, why don't you date?"

He toyed with his spoon. "I have no desire to repeat what happened with my ex-wife. And I'm just not that comfortable around women."

"Okay, the first one I get, but I call bullshit on the second."

His eyes widened. "What?"

"I've seen you flirt. You do just fine."

"Flirting is different. It's a woman's need to talk all the damn time that makes me uncomfortable."

"What, so you just want a fuck buddy? Wham, bam, thank you ma'am?"

Brady's cheeks reddened further. "Jesus, Macy. It's not like that. You make me sound like some kind of man-whore." He shifted in his chair. "I just like my peace and quiet, okay? Relationships take that away."

"If it's with the right woman, you won't care."

"Well, then, I guess I haven't dated the right woman."

"Have you tried?"

He spooned another mouthful of chili into his mouth and refused to answer. Truth be told, he hadn't. Peyton's betrayal cut deep. He never wanted to feel that way again. Like he was trash. Something convenient, then thrown away once he outlived his usefulness.

"It doesn't matter. I have no desire to be in a relationship." He stuffed the last of his cornbread in his mouth and stood. "Those cookies in the back?"

She sighed and nodded.

He picked up his bowl and beat a hasty retreat. His escape was short-lived, though. Macy followed him a minute later with her own empty dishes.

"If you did want a relationship, what would you want in a woman?"

He snatched a cookie off the baking tray and took a bite. Why did she insist on having this conversation?

"Why do you care? Planning to set me up? Because that will go nowhere real quick."

She sauntered closer, a naughty quirk to her lips, sending his defenses higher. What was she playing at?

"Maybe I'm just curious." She picked up a cookie and took a bite.

That was entirely plausible. If Macy was a cat, she'd have used several of her nine lives by now. But the look in her eyes and the set to her shoulders said there was something else at play.

"Macy." His voice held a note of warning.

She rolled her eyes. "I just don't understand it. You're a

nice guy. Successful, funny, smart. Sexy. You should be out looking for Miss Right and making mini-Bradys."

He choked on the bite of cookie. Damn, she didn't mince words. Coughing, he thumped his chest and cleared his throat. "You sound like Mom. Making mini-Bradys isn't high on my priority list. My siblings are handling the next generation of Archers just fine."

She ate another bite of her cookie as she stared at him. Her tongue darted out to lick away a bit of stray chocolate. He bit back a groan and shifted, trying to ease the sudden pressure in his pants.

A wicked grin spread over her face, and his eyes shot to hers. She'd caught him looking at her mouth. *Fuck*!

She took a step closer. Close enough he could touch her.

"I'm not the only one with chocolate on their face." She snaked a hand up and swiped at his bottom lip.

The instant she touched him, electricity shot down his spine. His muscles froze as he stared at her. Her eyes locked on his, their pupils large. She slid her hand along his jaw.

His hand landed on her waist, and he shifted closer. Her fingers slid into his hair on the back of his neck, her nails scratching the skin beneath, sending more bolts of lightning through him. He knew it wasn't wise, but he couldn't help himself. He tugged on her waist, sending her crashing into his larger frame.

Her hands curled into his shirt over his chest. His wrapped around her waist. They stared at each other, desire flaring. Like a magnet pulling him closer, he leaned down and lowered his mouth to hers.

Brady's heart stuttered at the feel of her lips under his. All his reasons for wanting to stay away flew out of his mind as he drank her in. She tasted like chocolate with a hint of spice. And of something uniquely Macy. She tasted like heaven. Like something he'd given up hope of ever finding again after he discovered his wife cheated on him and only married him for his money.

That thought drove him out of her arms. No. He didn't do relationships. Not anymore.

"I'm sorry," he said, his voice low. "I shouldn't have done that."

She cleared her throat. "I'm not complaining."

He wasn't, either. But that didn't mean he was going to do it again. No matter how tempting he found her. "I should go. It's getting late, and I have to be up early."

"I remember," she mumbled under her breath.

"Thanks for dinner and the cookies."

"You're welcome. Thanks for fixing my espresso machine. Take some of those with you." She pointed at the cookies.

He grabbed a napkin from the shelf behind him and wrapped several in it. "Thanks. I'll see you later." He didn't wait for her to say goodbye. Just made a beeline for the door to the café. He needed to get out of here before he let the memory of their kiss tempt him to do more.

FOUR

Arms full, Macy kicked the car door closed, then walked up Tara and Jace's drive to the front door. She used her foot to knock, then waited. The door swung open. Jace, hair disheveled and only socks on his feet, gave her a tired smile.

"Macy. Hi, come in."

She stepped inside, and he shut the door.

"Here, let me take that." He took the bags and box of diapers from her. "What is all this?"

Macy took off her coat and hung it up. "I went shopping." She'd made a trip to Colorado Springs and found a baby boutique. Tara and Jace's twins were going to be the best dressed babies in Silver Gap.

"Did you leave anything at the store?" Jace set the bags and diapers down on the dining table to her left and looked inside the sacks.

"There were a few things left when I was done." She smiled and walked over. "I know you guys didn't buy many clothes since you didn't know what you were having." She shrugged. "I know she didn't get many at her shower, either.

Just some unisex onesies." She grinned. "They're decked out now."

Jace pulled a frilly dress from one sack and laughed. "Oh, this is great. Tara will love this."

"Where is she, anyway?"

"In the babies' room, feeding them. It's naptime."

The trill of a phone broke the quiet. Jace reached into his pocket for his cell and looked at the screen. "It's Brady. Hang on." He swiped to answer. "Hello?"

His face morphed from residual amusement to concern and exasperation. "Of course he did. Okay. I'm on my way."

"What's wrong?" she asked as he hung up.

"Elbert jumped the fence. I need to go help look for him." He walked to the kitchen and scooped his truck keys from the counter before heading for the garage door. "Let Tara know where I went? I'll be back soon."

"Jace."

He paused with his hand on the knob and looked back.

"I think you're forgetting something?"

He frowned. "What?"

Macy pointed at his feet, trying not to laugh.

He glanced down, then snorted. "Christ. I'd forget my head right now if it wasn't attached."

"How about you stay here and take a nap with the twins? I'll go help look for Elbert."

His eyes darted toward the bedrooms, indecision in his eyes. "I might be the only one he'll come to, though."

Crap. She hadn't thought of that. "Okay, then. How about I drive? You go put some boots on while I tell Tara what's happening."

"I'm only going to the barn. I can drive that far in my sleep-deprived state." He turned to the pile of shoes to the side of the door, plucking his boots out even as he protested.

"Humor me." She spun on her heel. "I'll be right back." She headed around the corner and down the hall to poke her head into the nursery.

Tara glanced up from feeding one of the twins when the door opened, smiling as she saw Macy. "Hi." Her voice was barely a whisper.

"Brady called," she whispered back. "Elbert escaped. Jace and I are going to help look for him."

"That damn horse. Some days, I think he's more trouble than he's worth."

"Probably. You going to be okay here alone?"

"Yeah." She waved a hand. "Go find his ornery ass."

"I left you some things on the dining table. Baby stuff. We'll be back." Macy waved and closed the door, returning to the kitchen.

Jace had his boots on and a jacket. He'd run his fingers through his hair as well.

"You look more human. Let's go." She headed for the front door.

He let out a snort. "I don't feel it. I forgot what it was like to have a newborn. Times two is even worse."

Macy laughed and climbed into her car. "You wouldn't trade it for anything, though."

"No, I wouldn't." He buckled his seatbelt as Macy put the car in gear and backed out of the driveway.

"Where am I going?"

"Brady said the horse barn."

She pointed the car in that direction, butterflies in her stomach. She had an ulterior motive for wanting to come along. It had been a week since Brady fixed her espresso machine and kissed her senseless. She hadn't seen or heard from him since. But a meeting between them needed to happen. The longer they went without seeing each other, the more she was sure he would withdraw from her and things would grow awkward. For the sake of her friendships with his siblings and in-laws, that couldn't happen.

Macy turned off the lane that ran in front of the houses and onto the gravel drive to the barn, pulling to a stop out front next to several trucks. They got out and went inside. As her eyes adjusted to the interior, she saw Brady standing with Lee and several of the ranch hands.

She knew the moment he spotted her with Jace. His words faltered and he stiffened. He locked eyes with her for a split second before looking away. Macy's mouth flattened. It looked like he was just going to pretend she wasn't there. They'd see how long that lasted. She'd make sure it wasn't very long.

Jace walked up to the group, and Macy followed. She crossed her arms and made sure she was in his line of sight. His eyes darted to her again before he looked over the group.

"What's the plan?" Jace asked.

"We're going to split into teams of two on horseback to look for him," Brady said.

"You're sure he jumped the fence?"

"Unless someone snuck onto the ranch and stole him without us seeing, yes. But he was here this morning. I let him and the others out into the pasture, then went to do some chores. Dad stopped in the barn to get his horse and noticed Elbert missing. There were people all over this morning, so I doubt anyone took him. We'd have noticed someone leading him away. If they could even get close enough to do so."

"Okay. There's eight of us, so four teams of two? One team going in each direction?" Jace said.

Brady nodded.

Macy stepped next to Brady. "I'm riding with you."

He looked down at her, his eyes wide. "What? No. You can ride with Dad."

She glanced at Lee, who had an amused twinkle in his eyes, then back at Brady. "As nice as that would be, you and I need to talk."

"No, we don't."

"Yes, we do. It's about my espresso machine."

Twin pops of color bloomed on his cheeks above his beard. He cleared his throat. "I'm sure it can wait. We have a horse to find."

"Which will take lots of riding. Where we have nothing better to do than talk as we look." She turned her attention to the hands. "Partner up and let's go. Elbert's just getting further away the more we stand here."

They stared at her, unsure about taking directions from her. Lee clapped his hands. "You heard the lady. Get on your horse and get going. Jace, you can ride with me. Everyone make sure you take a sat phone."

Macy smiled her thanks at him as the group dispersed.

Lee walked past her, stopping to tip his head close. "I sure hope you know what you're doing."

She patted his arm. "I do."

He cast a glance up at his son, then walked away, leaving her alone with Brady. She looked up at him. He stared at her, his brown eyes glittering in the barn lights as his jaw worked beneath his beard. Without a word, he spun on his heel, heading for his horse, Titan.

Macy followed. "What horse do you want me to ride?"

"I don't care. Just pick one. Meet me in the corral when you've got it saddled." He opened the stall door, his words clipped.

She rolled her eyes and wandered down the aisle, looking for a suitable horse to ride. Tara's chestnut mare, Brandywine, stuck her head over the stall door and whickered.

"Hey, girl." She rubbed the horse's head and scratched her

ears. "You want to go for a ride? Find that stubborn, crazy friend of yours?"

Brandywine snorted and bobbed her head. Macy giggled. "Okay. Let's go." She grabbed a lead rope and the horse's halter from the hook by the door, then opened the stall. Murmuring to the horse as she went, she slid on the halter, buckling it, then snapped on the lead rope and led Brandywine from her stall to the tack room.

Thankful she and Tara were close to the same size, she found Tara's saddle and Brandywine's bridle and readied the horse, keeping one eye on Brady, who stood just outside the barn doing the same to Titan. She wouldn't put it past him to take off without her. He clearly did not want to talk.

Once she finished saddling her horse, she headed outside, where Brady fiddled with the straps on Titan's saddle, checking and rechecking the fit.

He glanced at her. "About time."

Macy narrowed her eyes at him. "Be happy I can saddle my own horse. I'm just slower than you because I don't do it every day." She rolled her eyes again and went to put her foot in the stirrup to mount up.

"Wait."

She paused and looked at him. He walked over and nudged her back.

"I want to double check your saddle."

Macy huffed. "Just because I don't ride as much as you, doesn't mean I don't know how to saddle a horse."

"Humor me." He threw her words back at her.

She crossed her arms and cocked a hip, waiting for him to declare her ready to go. "Have at it."

He tossed a look at her from the corner of his eyes, but said nothing as he tugged on the belly strap and checked Brandywine's bridle.

"Looks good."

"Duh." She took the reins from him and mounted the horse, grateful she'd worn jeans and sneakers to the ranch. "Can we go now?"

"Hey, you're the one who invited yourself on this operation." He swung into the saddle.

Macy's mouth went dry. Brady on the ground was impressive with his height and thick, muscular build, but on the back of a horse he was like a god sitting atop his steed, ready to go into battle. She could just see him in leather pants, shirtless, as he rode across the plains.

She shifted in her saddle and turned her horse toward the open pasture. "So, where are we headed?"

He pointed ahead of them. "The trail to the river."

"Did you get a satellite phone?"

"It's in my saddlebag. I have water for us as well."

"Awesome. Let's go." She squeezed Brandywine's sides, and the horse took off at a slow canter.

They rode across the pasture and through the back gate to go up the trail on the other side. Macy kept her head on a swivel as they went, looking for any sign of the silver horse.

"How are we going to find him? He could be anywhere."

"Thomas put the drone in the air. We're spread out, so hopefully no one's too far away once he spots him. *If* he spots him. There's a lot of wooded land on the Broken Bow."

Macy glanced around. "Yeah, but it's further away from the buildings. Before you pass the river, it's more open."

"Right. I still don't see him, though."

"I'm hoping he went up toward the lake. Jace and Tara go up there a lot, so he might head there. I sent Jace that way."

"Has he ever jumped the fence before?"

"He used to on a fairly regular basis, but he stayed close. He hasn't since Jace started riding him. But they haven't been going out much the last month or so, and Jace hasn't been in the barn at all in the week since the twins arrived."

"So, he's acting out because he misses his master."

"Pretty much."

That made sense. Elbert was a handful on a good day, and only Jace could keep him in line. He and the horse had a bond like no other.

They continued on the trail to the river, stopping here and there to listen for the sound of a horse crashing through the brush, but it was quiet. Only birds and wind and the occasional bellow of a cow broke the silence.

The tension between them grew thicker as they rode. Macy kept casting glances at him to find him doing his damnedest to pretend she wasn't there. When he noticed her watching him, he would ride ahead and ignore her. She would catch up and he would do it again. Finally, she had enough. She rode forward and swung Brandywine into his path, forcing him to stop.

"Macy, what the hell?"

"Stop ignoring me."

"I'm not ignoring you. I'm looking for Elbert."

"Bullshit. You won't even look at me."

"Because you aren't Elbert. Can't find the horse if I'm looking at you."

"Normal people look at each other some when they talk."

"We weren't talking."

"Exactly."

"Huh?" He sighed and pinched the bridge of his nose. "What the hell are you talking about? I'm confused."

Macy rolled her eyes. "Men," she muttered under her breath, then sighed. "You won't talk to me and you won't look at me. Why? And don't tell me it's because you're looking for Elbert," she said when he opened his mouth to speak. "Stop using him as an excuse."

"I didn't want to ride with you to begin with. Why should I talk to you?"

Ouch. That was harsh.

"You're avoiding me. You like me and don't want to admit it. Well, guess what? I like you too, and I'm not afraid to say so."

"Macy—"

"If you're going to deny it, don't say anything."

He held up a finger. "I think anything I have to say is irrelevant right now except what you want to hear. That being said, I won't deny I find you attractive. I think our kiss the other night proved that. But it's not going any further. You can rail at me until you blow smoke out your ears; it won't change my mind."

"Really? So, even if I stripped naked right here, you'd just ride on?"

Heat flared to life in his eyes and she grinned, knowing she'd gotten at least some reaction from Mr. I'm Always In Control.

He swallowed hard and glanced away for a moment. "Please don't. I—damn. I just can't, okay? Can we leave it at that?"

She arched a brow. "Can't or won't? They're very different." She spun Brandywine around. "I think it's the latter." Macy let the horse carry her toward the river as tears threatened. Stupid, stubborn, *infuriating* man. Why couldn't he let himself feel what his heart and body wanted to feel? Why did he have to resist it? If the strength of her own feelings was anything to go by, they could have something amazing and special. But no. He had to be a chickenshit.

Pissed off and stuck in her head, she almost missed the pile of horse poop to her right. In fact, she rode right past it. But it registered as she passed, and she pulled Brandywine to a halt.

"Brady, look." She pointed at the fresh pile.

He reined Titan in beside her. "It looks like he walked that way. There's a hoof print there. And there." He pointed to the dirt leading away from them. "Come on." He sent Titan in that direction, scanning the ground for more signs of the runaway horse.

They rode at a steady trot, seeing the occasional print or broken branch from Elbert's path. Brady called the others with an update and their location in the hope they could locate the horse by air with the drone and box him in.

"How far ahead of us do you think he is?"

"An hour? Maybe less? He probably meandered to the river, then doubled back. He's headed up the mountain now, probably on his way to the lake. He can't be that far away. He only had a couple hours head start to begin with."

Brady's phone trilled from the saddlebag. He fished it out and answered it.

"Yeah?"

Macy stared at him as he listened.

"Okay, we'll head that direction." He hung up.

"Well?"

"Thomas found him. He said he's about a mile that way." He pointed ahead and to the left.

Macy didn't wait. She kicked her heels into Brandywine's sides and took off. Brady and Titan kept pace. After about five minutes, he signaled for her to slow down.

"We're probably close. Let me call Thomas back and find out what he sees."

Macy nodded, but didn't look at him, scanning through the trees instead. A flash of silver caught her attention.

"There!" She flapped an arm at Brady, then pointed ahead to her right. "What's that? Damn, it disappeared."

He paused with the phone in his hand to look where she indicated. They both held their breath, waiting to see if what she saw came back. Something light flitted through the thick foliage.

"I think that's him." Brady put the phone away and sent Titan into a quick canter.

Macy followed. As they got closer, she caught a glimpse of Elbert's head. He was on a tear, heading south toward the river.

"Shit. We need to cut him off. We rose in elevation and there's a steep drop to the river. I'm not sure he can run down it at that speed." He nudged Titan into a full gallop.

Macy's heart leaped into her throat. They would never catch up. Elbert was the fastest horse on the ranch.

Titan was no slouch, though. He pulled ahead of her to the point she only caught glimpses of him and Brady as they moved through the dense forest. She heard Brady shout and the loud whinny of a horse. Heart thundering in her ears, she bent low and urged Brandywine to go faster. When she finally caught up, it was to see Brady at the top of the rise, a rope strung from his saddle pommel to something below. Titan dug his hooves in and backed up, but made little progress.

She stopped next to him several yards away and looked down. The rope was around Elbert's neck, but he fought Brady's effort to bring him back up.

Macy didn't think. She jumped off Brandywine, letting her reins trail on the ground, and slid down the embankment.

"Macy! What the fuck are you doing?"

She didn't answer him. Instead, she maneuvered herself to the rope strung taut between the horses and grabbed ahold, wrapping it around her forearm. "Release the rope!"

"What? Are you nuts? He'll drag you."

"No, he won't. He's fighting the control. Let go." She looked up. "Trust me?"

He closed his eyes, muttering to himself, then opened them again. "Fine." He unwound the rope from his pommel and let it slide free of his hand.

She kept her hand open, letting it slip over her arm as Elbert sidestepped several paces as the tension released, only grabbing on again once he danced in place. It slid over her palm, leaving behind a rope burn. She hissed, wishing she'd worn gloves, but didn't let go. Elbert danced and tossed his head. Macy gave him a little slack, but walked forward, murmuring to him as she went. His bright blue eyes were wide. Sweat slicked his silvery hide and he knickered nervously.

"Shh. It's okay. We're going to take you back to the barn. I bet there will be an apple waiting. And Jace. You want to see your buddy, don't you? He's out looking for you, too, you silly horse."

Elbert's ears twitched, but he stayed still. Macy edged closer, sliding her hands up the rope. Three feet from his head, he let out a loud neigh and shook his head. She froze, not wanting to spook him. He extended his neck to sniff her, his warm breath fanning her face. She reached out a hand to pet his muzzle. He let her touch him and stepped closer.

She let out a sigh of relief and moved in to stroke his neck. "That's it, big guy. Let's go home, huh?"

"Well, shit. I thought Jace was the only one who could do that."

Macy smiled, but kept her eyes on Elbert. "I sneak him treats when I visit. He saved Tara, after all."

"Of course you do. Okay, horse whisperer. Can you get him back up here?"

"We can try, right Elbie?" She rubbed his head and took hold of the rope near his neck, trying to walk him up the hill. He balked, pulling against the rope. She gave him some slack. "Okay, okay. You don't want to be led. How about a ride, then? Will you let me ride?" She smoothed a hand along his neck and over his withers, putting her other hand on his rump.

"What are you doing? Woman, I swear..."

"Hush. It's this or we wait for Jace and hope Elbert lets him ride, because he wants nothing to do with this rope."

"Macy…"

She glanced up at him. "I know what I'm doing. Tara and I rode bareback all the time as teenagers."

"I remember. But you never rode a horse like Elbert without a saddle."

"First time for everything." She inched her hand forward to tangle in Elbert's mane, grabbing on and tugging, getting him ready for her to use it as leverage to mount and then hold on. He stayed still.

"Okay, you big lug. Don't toss me, please." Saying a prayer, she gripped his mane and jumped, throwing her right leg over him while using her left hand in his mane to pull herself up. He took a few steps to the side and neighed, but didn't rear. She wiggled into position on his back and eased up, so she sat straight. "All right." A bright smile lit her face, and she looked at Brady. He shook his head, but a grin tugged at one corner of his mouth.

"It's probably too steep for you to ride him up here bareback. Meet me down river?"

She nodded. "You have Brandywine?"

"I'll tie her to me. We're good."

Macy urged Elbert to turn. The horse responded to her tap on his neck and the pressure from her thighs and they were on their way, picking over the uneven ground near the river. Several times, she slipped and nearly fell into the water as the horse picked up his pace, but she managed to hang on by the grace of God. She vowed never to skip leg day again.

~

Arms laden with Titan's tack, Brady did his best to ignore Macy's musical laugh. She stood with Jace near Elbert's stall.

He walked past them to the tack room, keeping his eyes straight ahead. They were back at the ranch, Elbert safe in the barn once more. He'd trotted to his stall and stuck his face in his grain bucket like nothing happened. Blasted horse. Not only did the hunt pull Brady away from his other chores—chores he still had to do—but it also brought him face-to-face with Macy. He'd done a damn good job of avoiding her since the night he fixed her espresso machine and screwed the pooch by kissing her. It had been a week and he still couldn't get the taste of her out of his mind.

He put Titan's saddle on the rack with a little more force than necessary, and the entire unit rattled.

"Careful, or you going to create more work for yourself."

The sound of Macy's husky contralto stiffened his muscles. "It slipped." With careful movements, he lifted his right hand to hang Titan's bridle on its hook.

"Uh-huh, sure." She stopped next to him, her thumbs hooked in her belt loops.

"What do you want?"

"You know what? Forget it." She spun around to walk away.

Brady's conscience kicked in. His hand shot out to grab her arm before she could get far. Startled, she looked back at him.

"I'm sorry. That was rude." And it was. His mom would tan his hide if she saw him behave that way. He let go of her arm. "Did you need something?"

She watched him for several moments, those indigo eyes studying him. He fought the urge to squirm.

"I just wanted to ask if you needed any help with your chores. I know you're behind now."

Shame at his rudeness flooded him. He didn't deserve her kindness. "It's not the first time an animal has put me behind. It won't be the last. I can handle things."

"I'm sure you can, but I'm just saying you don't have to."
She held out her hands. "I don't have anything to do tonight. I
was just going to visit with Tara and the twins, but I can do
that anytime. Put me to work."

His first instinct was to tell her no. But then he remembered the ranch books waiting for him. Macy was great with
numbers. "You feel like balancing the ranch books? I hate
doing it, and so do Mom and Dad."

"Sure. Where is everything?"

"At my house. Come on. I'll drive you over there."

"I can walk. Just give me your house key."

"You sure? It'll only take a couple minutes to take you over
there."

"I'm sure. You have other things to do here." She held out
a hand, palm up. "Key, please."

He took his keys from his pocket and found the house key,
removing it from the ring. "This is for the front door. I don't
know what time I'll be back. Lock up and leave that on the
kitchen counter if I'm not home before you're done. The
receipts and invoices are all on my desk. We use a spreadsheet
to track expenses. It's on my computer."

"Okay. Is there anything I should know?"

"A few of the invoices need paid. Can you write the checks
and leave them out for me to sign?"

"Yep."

"Thanks, Macy. That actually really helps a lot."

She offered him a soft smile. "You're welcome. I'll see you
later."

He nodded and waved as she turned around and sauntered
out of the tack room. Once she disappeared from view, he
scrubbed his hands over his face and groaned. What the hell
was he going to do about her? Ignoring her wasn't working.
He had zero desire to go find another woman. He didn't want
a relationship, but casual sex with her was not an option. He

was sure it would backfire on him, anyway. Sex with Macy promised to be epic. A brief fling would never cut it.

But what did that leave him with?

"A fucking mess, that's what." He groaned again and walked out of the tack room to finish his chores. Maybe if he took his time, she'd be gone when he got home.

FIVE

The lock on Brady's front door clicked as Macy let herself inside. It wasn't the first time she'd been there alone. It was just as weird now as it was before. The entire time she lived with him when she moved out here for protection, she felt like an invader. He grunted and grumbled at her whenever she tried to talk to him, then retreated to his bedroom with a book. Nothing had really changed.

She locked the door behind her, then headed down the hall to his office. She stepped inside and sat down in the leather chair behind the large mahogany desk. A glance at the surface had her sighing. There were piles all over. She was sure he knew what they all were, but she hadn't a clue.

Well, nothing to do but get started. She pulled the first pile toward her and began sifting through it.

His organization system was actually pretty straightforward. She had no trouble understanding it once she went through everything. She made a mental note to get him one of those stackable paper trays. For a man who was so organized in everything else, she didn't know why he didn't have one.

It took her a little over an hour to write checks, input

invoices into the ranch's accounting spreadsheet, and make sure everything balanced. Once she was done, she pushed away from the desk and stood, stretching. She scanned the room as she did so, noting the layer of dust on the shelves. It looked like he hadn't cleaned in a while.

She made her way out of the office to the closet in the kitchen where he kept his cleaning supplies and found a rag and the dust spray, going back to the office to spruce it up. That led her to the living room, which was equally dusty, then the rest of the house.

By the time she finished, she'd worked up a sweat and decided to keep going. She dragged the floor duster out and swept all the floors, then mopped them, vacuuming the carpet last.

As she moved from room to room, she noted the full hamper in his bedroom and started a load of laundry, then finally ended up in the kitchen where she unloaded the dishwasher and started another load before opening the freezer to see what she could make for dinner. It had grown dark a couple hours ago, and she was starving. Wrapped packets of meat greeted her. She rooted through to familiarize herself with what was available, then went into the pantry.

"Jackpot." She grabbed a jar of salsa, taco seasoning and a package of tortillas, then went back to the freezer to get the ground beef she saw. She'd make tacos.

While the meat defrosted in the microwave, she took a head of butter lettuce from the fridge and washed and diced it, setting it aside for later. By then, the meat was thawed enough to cook, so she put it in a skillet and lit the stove, turning the flame to just over medium. The scent of cooking meat soon filled the kitchen. She'd just added the seasoning when the door from the garage into the laundry room opened and Brady walked in.

"Hi. I hope you're hungry." She peered through the kitchen door and smiled at him.

He paused in the doorway a moment, staring at her, before stepping forward to shut the door. "I am. You didn't have to cook for me." He toed off his boots and came inside.

She shrugged and stirred the meat. "After I finished your books, I cleaned some. This place was a mess. Do you never clean? About the only thing that wasn't filthy was your bathroom. Anyway, I worked up an appetite, so I found stuff to make tacos."

"You cleaned my house?"

She nodded. "Get a couple plates out, would you? This is ready."

He moved into the kitchen and took down two plates. "You didn't have to clean anymore than you had to cook."

She shrugged again. "Like I said, it was a mess. You need a housekeeper."

"Yeah, well, forgive me if I'm a little leery of inviting a stranger into my house after all the weird shit that's happened in the last year."

"Truth. How many tacos do you want?"

"Three or four. However many we have meat for."

She handed him four tortillas and took two for herself, filling them with the taco meat, then moving out of his way. "You can have the rest." She added toppings to her tacos, then set her plate on the table before going back to get a bottle of water.

"You want some?" She held up a bottle. He nodded, so she took a second one from the fridge and went back to the table.

He finished making his tacos and folded his long frame into a seat across from her. "Thanks for dinner."

"You're welcome." She took a bite of her taco and tried not to stare at him as she ate. He'd left his hat on a hook in the laundry room and ran a hand through his hair. It was a disheveled mess, but sexy as hell. Dark locks with a few streaks of silver curled over his forehead and teased the collar of his shirt. Macy wanted to comb her fingers through it.

"Did the books balance?"

She swallowed the food in her mouth and nodded. "Yes. It was all fine."

"Good."

They finished eating in silence. The scrape of her chair's legs on the tile floor felt unnaturally loud as she stood up to put her plate in the dishwasher. He followed her with his own. Macy stepped back to give him access to the machine. He put his plate next to hers, then shut the door and straightened.

"Thanks again for supper. It was good."

"You're welcome. I should probably get going. It's late and we both have an early morning."

"Yeah. You have, um, something..." He touched the side of his mouth.

Macy swiped at her cheek. She had food on her face? Of course she did. Nothing ever went smoothly around Brady. "Did I get it?"

He shook his head. "No, it's further to the left."

She tried again.

He smiled. "The other left. Here, let me." He reached out and touched her cheek with his thumb.

Macy stilled as he made contact. His hand lingered, his fingers skimming her face. Her breath caught as he trapped her with his gaze. In their dark depths, longing warred with his desire to walk away. He closed them for a brief moment, uttering a curse before he stepped forward and took her face in his hands to kiss her.

She balled her fists in his shirt and held on for dear life as he plundered her mouth, stealing her breath. When his hands traveled south to wrap around her waist, she let go and did what she wanted to do all through dinner. His hair was cool and silky beneath her fingers.

The room spun as he lifted her off her feet and pressed her against the wall. His mouth left hers to trail fire along her jaw and down her neck. She sucked in some much needed air. It was full of his musky scent and only enhanced the pleasure he created as he kissed his way down her throat. When he palmed her breast through her shirt, she moaned.

It was the catalyst he needed to let go of the reins holding back his desire. His hands tugged her shirt up her torso, yanking it over her head to bare her lace-covered breasts. With deft fingers, he unsnapped the back closure on her bra and the material fell away. His mouth took its place.

Macy tunneled her fingers into his thick hair. Her head thunked against the wall, need mounting deep inside her as he kissed and laved her breasts with his mouth. Feeling the reins of her control slipping, she tugged him back to her lips and latched on, giving as good as she got. He palmed her ass with his big hands, pulling her flush against his fly. She moaned into his mouth and ground against him before unbuttoning his shirt and tugging it free of his jeans. The soft cotton of his undershirt met her fingertips. She broke away to growl.

"You're wearing too many clothes."

"So are you." With a flick of his wrist, he unsnapped her pants, sliding his hands beneath the fabric to whisk them and her panties down her legs. She stepped out of them and kicked them away.

Macy pulled at his shirt. He drew it over his head, tossing it aside. Her mouth watered as she got a glimpse of his muscular chest and tattooed arms. She raked her hands through his springy chest hair. His arms went around her waist, trapping her against him. The coarse hair tickled her bare breasts, sending fiery tentacles of heat through her body.

She wiggled, tucking her arms between them to get to his

fly as he took her mouth, his tongue sampling every corner. When her hand brushed the hard ridge behind the denim, his muscles tensed for a fraction of a second before she found herself rising up the wall, her feet six inches from the floor. He pulled her legs around his waist, then freed himself from the confines of his pants.

His hot shaft teased her entrance. A wave of pleasure rocketed through her.

He groaned. "Need a condom."

"I'm on the pill." She rocked her hips, taking the tip of him inside.

"Fuck." His head rolled back, exposing the cords of his neck.

Macy leaned forward and nipped at them. "Yes, please."

He cradled her hips in his hands and slid deeper. She hissed as he stretched her.

"More, Brady."

He pushed forward, seating himself. "I hope you don't want slow, because that's not gonna happen."

"Do your worst." She brought his mouth to hers. Their tongues dueled as he pulled back, then drove home. Sandwiched between him and the wall, she rode him hard, the angle hitting all the right spots to send her sailing over the top. She screamed his name as she came, flying apart into bright shards of intense heat and light.

As the pleasure rolled over her, he continued to pound into her body, seeking his own release. Macy felt another orgasm build from the ashes of the first. She tightened her legs around him, squeezing her inner muscles. He buried his face in her neck, biting the juncture of her shoulder as he pumped faster. Her second climax hit on the heels of his, taking them both to the stratosphere.

Bones liquified, her legs dropped, and she slid down his body, only his hands on her hips keeping her from sinking to the floor in a pile of satisfaction. She clutched his biceps, leaning her face against his muscular chest, and smiled.

"I'm not sure I can walk. You might have to carry me to bed."

If she'd dumped a bucket of ice water on his head, she couldn't have gotten a stronger reaction. He released her so fast she had to lock her knees to stay upright. That kept her from falling long enough for her to lean into the wall.

He stepped back, tugging his pants up, and ran a hand through his hair, regret shining in his dark eyes.

Macy's euphoria died, bringing the starch back to her body. She pushed away from the wall.

"What? I'm good enough to screw against the wall, but not good enough to take to your bed?"

He closed his eyes, drawing in a deep breath. "Macy—"

"Save it." She bent over to gather her clothes. Anger made her movements jerky. Once she had everything, she straightened to level a glare on him. "I'm not interested in empty platitudes and excuses. One day, you're going to regret letting me walk away tonight. I hope it can keep you warm in that giant bed of yours." She stepped around him to go find the bathroom and dress. "Goodnight, Brady."

SIX

The trill of Macy's phone drew her away from the toaster and the bagel she waited on. Curious about who would call her at six in the morning, she spun the device around where it sat on the counter to see Declan's face on the screen. Worried, she picked it up and answered.

"Hey, everything okay?"

"Not exactly," he croaked.

Macy pulled the phone away to stare at it. His voice was an octave deeper than normal and scratchy. Her bagel popped up, so she put him on speaker and opened the cream cheese. "You sound sick. Are you sick?"

"As a dog. I think I have the flu." He punctuated his words with a wracking cough.

She slumped against the counter. Well, this put a wrench in things. "Damn. I guess we'll have to postpone our camping trip." They were due to leave in the morning with their younger sisters.

"I hate to do that. Maybe you can get one of Maggie's brothers to go."

An image of Brady the last time she saw him floated

through her head. It had been almost a week. Five days since he rocked her world against the kitchen wall, then broke her heart by looking at her as though he wished he'd never touched her. "Maybe. I'm not sure any of them can get away with such short notice."

"Just try. I don't want to disappoint the girls. They've talked about nothing else for weeks except this trip."

Macy knew that for the truth it was. Denise came in yesterday happy to be at work just so she didn't have to listen to them talk about sleeping in their brand-new sleeping bags and what animals they would see for the millionth time.

"I'll call around. But if none of them can get away, we'll have to do it another time."

"Okay. Yeah, I definitely don't think it's a good idea for the three of you to be out in the wilderness alone."

She didn't, either. She knew she could camp with them alone, but she would feel safer and more comfortable if there was another adult who had more wilderness experience than she.

"Me too. Okay, you get to feeling better, and if there's anything you need today, let me know."

"I think Maggie's got me covered, but I'll pass it along. Let me know what you decide to do."

"I will. Feel better, Deck." She said goodbye and hung up.

"Well, hell." She hung her head, contemplating what to do. Of the three Archer brothers, the only one who might be able to go was Brady. Thomas had a clinic with a schedule full of appointments, and Seb had a county to run, plus a pregnant wife. That left Brady. But he was as likely to say yes as she was to grow a third eye.

She let out a soft growl. Talking to him wasn't something high on her list. Spending a week in the wilderness with him was even lower, but she would do anything to make her sisters happy. She refused to disappoint them or Denise because Brady screwed her brains out, then left her high and dry.

Macy smeared cream cheese on her bagel, putting off the inevitable. Would he even answer if she called? Maybe she should drive out there and ask in person. That might be better. He couldn't just hang up on her if he was staring her in the face.

Plan decided, she ate her bagel, then headed to the coffee shop to open up. Once Denise arrived, she would let her know what was going on, then drive out to the Broken Bow and find Brady.

~

A light breeze blew, ruffling Brady's sweaty hair as he pulled on the fencing to secure it to the post. The sound of horse hooves pounding over the ground made him look up. His fingers slipped off the wire as he realized it was Macy, and he slammed his hand into the post. Cursing, he took off his glove to inspect his hand, shaking it to make the pain go away.

She pulled up beside him, her horse puffing out a breath as they came to a halt.

"What are you doing out here?"

"Hi, Brady. It's nice to see you too. Been a while." She dismounted and came to stand next to him.

He straightened to his full height, hoping to intimidate her into getting back on her horse and riding away. She didn't, though. She just smiled up at him. He held back a growl. He'd been doing his damnedest to forget about the other night. Even went to Colorado Springs a couple nights ago, hoping to find a woman to erase the memory of Macy's legs locked around him as he drove them both to a state of euphoric madness. It hadn't worked. He left the woman's place before his shirt came off, knowing she—or any other woman, for that matter—was a poor substitute for who he really wanted. But Macy could never be a fling, and he didn't want a relationship. It hurt too much when it went south. So, he went home and took care of himself, Macy's full breasts, pretty face, and sexy walk in his head as he showered.

"Sure. Hi. What are you doing out here?"

She huffed. "I need your help."

He crouched and grabbed the fencing again, needing to put some distance between them. "Your machine break again? How about I just buy you a new one and save us both the trouble?"

"It's not my espresso machine. Declan's sick."

He looked up. "Sick? How sick?"

"He has the flu."

"Weren't you supposed to—"

"Go on our camping trip tomorrow, yes."

He rose. "So, what do you need my help with?" He had a sneaking suspicion what she was going to say, but prayed it was anything else.

"Is there any way you can get away from the ranch and come with us?"

That's what he was hoping she wouldn't say. He looked away and stared at the landscape.

"Please, Brady? I wouldn't ask if I had any other option. Hannah and Jessie have been looking forward to this for weeks."

Brady frowned. Why did she do this to him? Not only did he not want to disappoint those girls, it also bothered him to no end that she felt like he was a last resort. She should be able to come to him with anything, anytime. Their attraction to each other really screwed things up.

His guilt, though, drove him to his decision. "Let me talk to Dad, but it shouldn't be a problem."

Her face lit up. "Really?"

"Yeah."

She squealed and threw her arms around him. Brady caught her to keep them both from toppling over at her exuberance.

"Thank you!" She looked up at him, and her smile died. Awareness lit in her eyes.

He swallowed and released her, stepping back. "I need to finish this fencing. I'll talk to Dad when I'm done."

She tucked a strand of that glorious hair behind her ear and tossed the reins over her horse's head. "I'll be at Declan and Maggie's getting camping equipment." She motioned toward the houses in the distance with a quick jerk of her head. Her brother moved into Maggie's house at the beginning of the year and sold his, both of them preferring the quieter ranch atmosphere.

He nodded. "I'll come find you."

She swung up into the saddle. "Thanks again, Brady."

"Yep." He offered her a short wave, and she rode away.

He watched her for a moment, then rested his head on his hands on the fence post and groaned. If he made it through the week without sleeping with her again, it would be a miracle.

Macy smiled as she listened to her sisters chatter in the backseat of the car while she and Brady finished loading her SUV. Their energy was infectious, helping counter her lack of caffeine this morning. She'd only had time for one cup.

Brady slid a plastic tub full of food into the back and closed the hatch.

"Is that everything?" she asked.

"I think so." He stared at the car, one finger ticking. She

could tell he was going over some mental list. He glanced at her. "We're good."

"Okay. Let's get this show on the road." She moved to the passenger door and got in, knowing he would want to drive. She was content to let him.

"Are we leaving?" Jessie asked.

"Yep," Macy replied.

Both girls cheered.

Macy chuckled and turned to Brady. "I think they're excited."

He flashed a smile and turned out of her neighborhood. They left town and wound up into the hills, past the ranch. She and Declan had thought about camping on the ranch, but they wanted more established hiking trails, knowing it would be easier on the girls. And Macy wanted access to showers. She was not a rough it kind of girl. Tent camping was really pushing her boundaries.

They made small talk and listened to Hannah and Jessie sing along to the radio and point out interesting things they saw. After a couple hours, Brady pulled into the campground. Macy ran into the office to check them in and came back out with a map a few minutes later.

"Let me see." Brady held out his hand, and she gave him the map. He studied it for a moment. "We're near the river. At least it's cool out. That location would be really buggy in the summer." He glanced at her, handing it back and putting the car in gear. "You're going to have a trek to the showers, though. Luckily, there's a restroom not far, but it's far enough I'll probably pee in the woods."

"I want to pee in the woods!" Jessie said, making them laugh.

"I'll use the bathroom, thanks," Hannah said.

"Me too." Macy smiled at her.

"Wimps." Brady's eyes danced with mirth.

"No. Practical. Peeing without a toilet as a girl is not easy. I'd rather not get pee in my shoes."

"Eww! Never mind. I don't want to pee in the woods anymore."

Brady looked at Jessie in the rearview mirror. "Oh, come on. I thought you were my ally."

"I am. But I'm using the toilet." Jessie put her hands up and shrugged.

Macy's mouth twitched as Brady gave the girl a mock frown.

"What did I do to get surrounded by girls?"

Macy laughed. "You'll survive." She patted his shoulder.

"But will I emerge unscathed?" He raised a brow. "We're here." He pulled into the short drive at their campsite and shut off the engine.

The girls scrambled out. Hannah opened the back hatch, and they each grabbed something.

"Whoa, whoa, whoa." Brady held out a hand. "Let's be careful about where we put things. The food needs to stay in the vehicle, so set it next to the car until we get the other stuff unloaded."

Both girls dropped their loads next to the wheel. He handed them sleeping bags. "Go set those on the picnic table."

They took off at a run.

"Well, they ought to go right to sleep tonight," he said as he watched them go.

Macy giggled and grabbed the camp chairs. "For sure."

Between the four of them, they unloaded the car in a few minutes. The girls opened the chairs and set up the table and canopy they brought while Macy and Brady worked on the tent.

"I'm glad you're tall. This thing's massive." She slid a pole through the slot, and he reached one long arm over to grab it and pull it to his side.

"I didn't even know we had this tent."

"You didn't. I bought it for this trip. I wanted us to have plenty of room, so we could move our chairs inside if it was too cold."

"Well, you accomplished your goal. I think you bought one of the largest tents on the market."

She slid another pole through. He took it and secured it on the other side. The tent was now semi-erect.

"Holy moly!" Jessie ran up beside her. "It's like a house!" She whipped around. "Hannah! Do you see this thing?"

Hannah giggled. "I see it."

"This is so cool!"

"Did you guys finish setting up the table and canopy?" Macy asked.

They nodded.

"Yep!" Jessie said.

"How about you go scrounge up some firewood, then?"

"Stay close," Brady said. "You don't want to get lost."

"Okay!" The little girl ran to the edge of their campsite, her older sister on her heels.

Macy shook her head. "I wish I had a tenth of her energy."

He laughed. "What do you mean? You do."

"No, I don't."

"Yes, you do. You're always perky."

She waved a hand. "That's just my personality. I'm bubbly."

"Bubbly?"

"What would you call it?"

"Hyper."

Macy tipped her head. "Yeah. I can see that." She smiled at him. "Thanks again for coming with me." She really appreciated that he dropped everything to come with her and her sisters. She also was thankful to Lee and the ranch hands for taking up the slack so he could. Macy made a mental note to take some gift cards out to the ranch for them all when they got back.

He returned her smile. "You're welcome."

While they finished putting up the tent, the girls amassed a pile of firewood that would last quite a while. Macy was glad. The nights would be cold. She was just glad there was no snow in the forecast over the next few days. It was supposed to rain, though. She hoped not too much. The model she saw this morning before they left showed some showers tomorrow with some locally heavier stuff.

Brady set the last tent pole, pounding the stake down with a rubber mallet, and straightened. "Home sweet home."

Jessie dove through the door, Hannah right behind her.

"This thing has rooms! I get this one!" Jessie said.

"You two have to share. We don't have enough air mattresses—or rooms—for you to get your own," Macy said.

Jessie's head popped out. "Does that mean you and Brady are sharing, too?"

Macy knew her cheeks were bright red, but she couldn't stop the flush as thoughts of their kitchen encounter flooded her mind. She would love a repeat, but she knew he was happy to have the two young chaperones sleeping nearby. She cleared her throat. "No. I'm going to share a room with you. Brady gets his own."

"That means we get the bigger one," Hannah said, having popped up behind her sister. "Come on, Jess. Let's get our stuff and get it set up."

The two of them scampered out of the tent.

"Take the twin mattress and one of the queens into our room. Brady gets the other queen." She tamped down her need to jump Brady's bones and sent an amused look his way as the kids ran in and out of the tent with their supplies. "We should probably go help them blow up those mattresses."

"Probably." Brady stared in the door. "Are we sure we want to enter their lair, though?"

Macy laughed. "No. But I don't want a half-inflated bed." She ducked through the doorway and heard him follow her.

The girls jabbered while they worked, making the menial task of setting up camp less dull. With the four of them working, they had things organized the way they wanted them in half an hour.

"What should we do now?" Macy asked, stepping out of the tent.

"Explore, duh."

Macy tapped Jessie on the nose. "Cheeky." She grinned. "Okay. Let's explore." She turned to Brady. "Oh, Master Guide, sir, where shall we go?" She curtsied low, making the girls giggle.

"Does this make you my lady?" He blushed as he realized how that sounded and looked at the kids. "How about we take the summit trail since the weather's nice today?"

"Yeah! Mom gave us a digital camera. We can take some great pictures from up there," Hannah said.

"All right, then. Get your jackets and use the restroom," Brady said. "And fair warning, you might end up having to pee in the woods."

Both of them made a face. One Macy was sure she was making as well. He laughed and spun away to go back into the tent.

"I'm going to load up a pack with supplies for us. Mace, you should take one, too, just in case something happens to mine." He reemerged with his empty pack, which was attached to an aluminum frame, and a smaller backpack, which he handed to her. "Take a first aid kit, some water, and a handful of protein bars and other snacks. You have a wet bag, too, right?"

She nodded, taking the backpack from him.

"Good. Throw some dry socks and a long-sleeve shirt each in it."

"Okay. Girls, go get me a pair of socks and a shirt while we go get food and water from the car."

They dove inside the tent, and Macy shook her head. "What are the chances we're going to be carrying them back to camp later?"

He grinned. "Pretty good. Hope you've been working out. Jessie's little, but she's solid."

Macy batted her eyes and smiled back. "What? A he-man like you can't carry them both?" She started for the car.

"Only if I don't want to walk like a normal human being tomorrow." He followed her.

She giggled. "That would be funny. I'll whittle you a walking stick. How about that?"

He laughed and opened the back of the vehicle. "I'd like to see you do that. You'd be like Granny Clampett."

"Nuh-uh. I'm Elly May all the way." She gave him a saucy smile, then dug into the food tub for protein bars.

"You're not enough of an airhead to be Elly May." He took the protein bars and cheese crackers she offered him.

"Not enough of? That mean I am somewhat?" She glanced at him out of the corner of her eye. His cheeks reddened and his lips pursed.

"That's not what I meant. I meant—hell, you know what I meant."

She giggled. "I know. I'm just teasing." She passed him some trail mix, then put several packets in her bag before putting the lid back on the tub. She added some water to her pack and made sure she had a first aid kit and some bear spray, then strapped it on.

"Are we ready?" he asked.

"I just need to get my jacket."

"Me too." They walked over to the tent, where both girls

had their jackets tied around their waists. They held out Macy's and Brady's jackets to them.

"Thanks." Macy took hers and looped it around her waist.

Brady gave Hannah a nod as he accepted his, tying it on under his pack. "All right, let's go."

They set off through the trees, Brady in the lead. The girls chattered like squirrels as they walked, pointing out birds and animal tracks. Macy took a breath of the cool, clean mountain air as she listened to them. She didn't realize how much she needed this trip until just now. She felt lighter, happier, out here without the pressures of running her café. Being a business owner was great; she loved it, but it sapped her mentally much more than she'd realized.

About halfway up, they stopped to eat the lunch Brady stowed in his pack. Peanut butter and jelly sandwiches, apples, and some of the cookies London made special for them. Macy wished it was a macaron, but she wasn't complaining about double-chocolate chunk.

"Brady?" Hannah said.

He looked at her.

"Why couldn't we bring horses and ride? This would be faster on a horse."

He gave her a soft smile. "Getting tired?"

She nodded. "Mostly my feet."

"I'm not tired," Jessie quipped. "My feet feel great!"

Brady smiled at her and ruffled her blonde hair. "That's because I don't think your feet have touched the ground. You've skipped the entire way." He looked at Hannah. "Horses take a lot of work and you need to be comfortable in the saddle for long periods of time to take them camping. You two need to get some more lessons under your belt. Maybe next summer we can go horse camping."

"Will you come?" Hannah asked her older sister.

"Sure. I love to ride." As a teen, she spent many a day in

the saddle with Tara, Rayna, and London, as well as Thomas and Declan. There were days she explored the ranch by herself, too. When she needed to get out of the house and away from her mom. Jenny and Lee always understood. She never knew for sure, but she had a feeling one of them trailed her when she went alone just to make sure she was safe.

"That sounds fun. Can I ride Elbert?" Jessie asked.

Brady laughed. "No. I think he's a bit too much horse for you. We'll leave him to Jace."

She pouted, then shrugged. "Fine. I guess Winnie will do. I like her. She's sweet."

"She is. And she'll keep you safe."

"That means she's slow," Hannah stage whispered to her sister.

Jessie scrunched her nose. "But I like to go fast."

"Not on a trail ride up the mountain," Macy said. "Those are meant to be slow. So you can enjoy yourself."

The little girl studied her. "I guess that makes sense. Okay." A chipmunk scampered across their path, and the girl took off toward it, sufficiently distracted from the topic of horses.

Macy finished her cookie and gathered up her trash as well as Hannah's and Jessie's and stowed it in a Ziploc bag, then stuffed it down into the bottom of her pack.

"You ready?" Brady asked.

She nodded, and he let out a sharp whistle to get the kids' attention. They came running back, and the four of them set off up the trail again. True to form, Jessie skipped ahead. Macy didn't know how she still had so much energy. She made a mental note to ask Denise if she gave her coffee this morning before she dropped them off. She pitied the girl's school teacher.

SEVEN

Brady glanced back at Macy to see her walking close to Hannah, their heads bent together as they talked. They were close to the tree line now, near the top of the mountain. He was proud of Jessie and especially Hannah for trekking so far. Jessie floated up the trail, while the slightly less energetic Hannah stuck close to her older sister, taking her time as she picked her way over the rocky terrain.

Noise drew his attention ahead, and he turned to see a black shape moving through the trees to their right. His amusement fled as he recognized the shape of a bear. He let out a whistle to get Jessie's attention. She spun around.

"Stay where you are," he called. "Don't move." He pointed to her right. "There's a bear over there. It's very important you stay put."

Her eyes grew large, and she slowly turned her head to look where he pointed. Brady edged closer, hoping he didn't alarm the bear by moving toward it instead of away, but he wasn't about to leave Jessie alone. With one eye on the bear and one eye on the girl, he moved toward her. Ten feet from her, the bear stood up and sniffed the air. Brady froze.

"Brady." Jessie's frightened whisper carried on the wind.

"It's okay. We're okay. I need you to take slow steps back toward me now. The bear doesn't want me to come any closer." It grunted at him, so he took a few steps back. He turned his head enough to see Macy from the corner of his eye. She and Hannah stood frozen twenty feet behind him. "Macy, get your bear spray ready." He didn't wait to see if she complied and found his own. He turned back to Jessie, who was a couple feet closer to him, but not as close as he'd like.

The bear sniffed the air again and let out a short grumble. Jessie whimpered as tears streamed down her face. When the animal dropped to all fours and ambled toward them, Brady took two long steps forward and scooped Jessie up. She turned her face into his neck and wrapped her legs around him the best she could with the pack he had on. The bear broke through the brush to stop a few feet away, bellowing.

Brady waved his free arm, making himself look bigger. The skinny black bear grunted again, studying him with its beady eyes. "Get out of here, bear!" He waved his arm again, even as he backed toward Macy and Hannah. It let out another bellow, but stayed put as he kept backing away.

He reached the others and nudged Macy back. "Walk backward. Don't take your eyes off the bear, but keep going."

They kept a steady pace down the trail until the bear was out of sight. Brady spun them all around, and they continued another hundred yards before he let them stop. He peeled Jessie off and set her feet on the ground. She clung to his arm.

"It's okay now, honey." He crouched in front of her and pushed her blonde bangs away from her face. "It's gone."

She looked around and sniffed. "I don't want to go to the summit now. I want to go back to camp."

He looked up at Macy, who nodded in agreement.

"Okay. We'll go back. That's probably a good idea. By the

time we'd find another way up to the top and then came back down, it would be getting dark. We'll make a yummy dinner over the fire and plan tomorrow's adventure, okay?" The girl nodded. Brady rose and started downhill, a more subdued Jessie still holding his hand.

The trek down took less time than the trip up, and they made it back in just over half the time. Jessie and Hannah retreated to the tent, while Macy and Brady walked toward the car to put away the food from their backpacks.

"Can you get dinner started? I'm going to go have a talk with the kids about wilderness safety. We should have done that before we set out."

Macy nodded. "Try to reassure them what happened isn't typical. I don't want them to be afraid the entire time we're out here."

He nodded. "I will."

She took his pack from him, and he walked over to the tent, pushing the flap aside to get in.

"Knock, knock." With a finger, he lifted the flap to the girls' room. They looked up at him from where they sat, their arms wrapped around their bent legs. He dropped to his knees in front of them and sat on the edge of Macy's mattress.

"You guys doing okay?"

They nodded, but he could see in their eyes they were still scared.

"I know what happened was scary, but seeing bears isn't common. They tend to avoid people. We're just as scary to them as they are to us."

"Really?" Hannah said.

"Really. And I want to apologize. I should have prepared you for the possibility of seeing a bear or some other large, scary animal. But we're going to rectify that right now and go over some wilderness safety. Okay?"

They nodded again.

"Okay. First thing. When you see a bear, freeze. Don't go any closer to it. Try to make yourself look bigger. If it doesn't run off, start backing away. Don't turn your back on it until you can't see it anymore. If it charges at you, throw stuff toward it. Sticks, rocks, whatever you can find. If it actually attacks you—and this is like a major what-if—you fight back with everything you have. Don't play dead. The most vulnerable points on any animal are the eyes, ears, and the throat. That includes humans."

Two pairs of solemn eyes stared at him.

"If it's a mountain lion, make yourself as big as possible. Don't bend down to pick anything up unless it's already charging you. If you need something to throw at it or wave at it, pull a branch off a tree, or pick up a rock on a boulder if there's one close. More than anything, be loud. And again, if it attacks, fight back."

They nodded.

"I don't want to scare you, but you need to be aware of the dangers of the woods. Colorado has some large predators. I want you to enjoy yourselves, though, and don't be too afraid to skip ahead and have fun. We're not likely to see another bear so close the whole trip, okay?"

He got nods again.

"Okay. Now, who wants to see if we can talk Macy into s'mores for dessert?"

Hands shot up.

"Me!" Jessie said.

He stood, promptly hitting his head on the top of the tent. That sent them into peals of giggles. He laughed with them.

"I guess I need to shrink a few inches." He stooped and walked out of the room. The kids followed him out, and they found Macy adding wood to the small fire she started in their fire ring. She looked up.

"What are you guys laughing about?"

"Brady hit his head on the tent ceiling," Hannah said.

"Really? That gigantic thing is too short for you?"

He shrugged and picked up a log, adding it to the fire. "Back there it was."

"How tall are you, anyway?" Jessie asked.

"Six-feet-seven-inches."

Her eyes turned to saucers. "Whoa."

Macy giggled. "And that's why he hits his head on tent ceilings."

"And low doorways." He smiled. "I've beaned myself pretty good a couple times. I usually remember to duck now."

"That's good." She pointed past him. "Can you put that grate over the fire? I think we can put the chicken on now."

He picked up the metal grate and set in on the stones around the fire. Macy took out several pre-seasoned chicken breasts and laid them on top. She wiped her hands with a kitchen wipe and rinsed them with a little water, then set several foil-wrapped ears of corn on the grate.

Jessie nudged him. When he looked at her, she crooked a finger, asking him to bend down, so he did.

"Ask about the s'mores," she whispered in his ear.

He gave her a solemn nod and straightened. "So, what's for dessert?"

Macy shot him an amused smile, her eyes flicking to her sisters before settling on him again. "We haven't even had dinner and you're wondering what's for dessert?"

"Well, yeah. It's the most important part of the meal."

She chuckled. "No argument there." She looked at the girls. "What do you guys want?"

"S'mores!" they said in unison.

"But not just any kind of s'mores," Brady said. "Campfire s'mores. With strawberries."

"You can do that?" Jessie said, awe in her voice and on her young face.

Macy laughed. "You can do anything you want to s'mores. Even add sprinkles."

If possible, the awe grew. The girl's mouth dropped open. Hannah giggled and gave her shoulder a nudge.

"Wow." Jessie's face lit up as she thought of something and she ran back into the tent, reemerging a moment later before they had a chance to really wonder what she was up to. She held up a deck of Uno cards. "Who wants to get their butt kicked while we wait for dinner?"

"Oh, those are fightin' words, little lady." Brady took the cards from her and headed for the picnic table. "I'll play you for the first s'more."

"You're on!" She settled across from him, Hannah coming to sit beside her.

Brady doled out the cards, ready to claim first dibs on dessert.

With a sigh, Macy sank into the cabin chair next to Brady in front of the fire.

"Kids all settled?"

She tugged her coat tighter and nodded. A yawn cracked her jaw. "Man, I should join them. I need to let the sugar wear off a bit, though. Why did you let me eat that last s'more?"

He shrugged. "You seemed like you were enjoying it."

Oh, she had. It was a good thing they were going to do so much hiking over the next few days. Despite her protests, she planned to eat as many s'mores as she damn well pleased.

"So," she yawned again, "what are we doing tomorrow?"

"The weather's supposed to be hit or miss, so I thought we

could go to the lake nearby and fish from the shoreline. If the girls pitch in, we can take our camp chairs and the canopy."

She giggled. "I can't wait to see Jessie's reaction to fishing. She's going to be bouncing around like mad, eager to catch one, then get bored while she waits, then imitate a jumping bean when she finally gets one."

He chuckled. "That's the truth. She's a spitfire. That will serve her well, though, as she gets older."

"Oh, I agree. No one's going to make her do anything she doesn't want to. I think I'm going to talk to Maggie about teaching her jiu jitsu. Both girls, actually. It'll not only give them a valuable skill, but help focus some of their energy, especially for Jessie."

"The boys in her class don't stand a chance."

"Nope."

They laughed, then fell into an easy silence as they sat by the fire, enjoying its warmth. Macy's body sank into the chair with every passing minute as the tension left her muscles and sleep edged its way in. She yawned and stretched.

"I should go change and get to bed. It's been a long day."

"Yeah, and tomorrow will be too." He stood and offered her a hand.

Macy took it, and he pulled her from the chair. Once on her feet, he didn't let go. She looked up and got caught in his dark gaze. Heat hotter than the fire behind him flared between them. She cleared her throat, but didn't look away.

"You were, um, really great with the kids today. A natural," she said.

He lifted one shoulder. "They're good kids. And I've had some practice lately with the kids Mom and Dad are fostering."

She tried to focus on his words, but he was running his thumb over her knuckles, distracting her. "Still, the way you helped Jessie get past being so scared—I'm glad you were here. Glad you *are* here."

"Yeah?" He shuffled closer.

Macy's breathing sped up. "Yeah."

The breeze blew a strand of hair over her face. He lifted his free hand and tucked it behind her ear, inching closer.

"Stop me, Macy. We shouldn't do this. It will only complicate things. More than they already are."

"I don't want to stop you." And she didn't. She wanted to complicate the hell out of stuff.

So she did. She stood on her toes and pressed her mouth to his. He let out a soft grunt of surprise, but didn't pull away. Feeling bold, she ran her tongue along the seam of his lips. He let go of her hand and pulled her into his body, taking over the kiss, sweeping inside her mouth. Macy returned the favor. She ran her hands up his shoulders into his hair, then down to furrow through his thick beard. She loved the feel of it beneath her fingertips. It was so soft.

He broke away to stare down at her, breathing hard. "Why do you do this to me?" He didn't give her a chance to answer, kissing her again. His hands dove under her jacket to roam her back. They were hot against her bare flesh. She let out a moan and curled her fingers into his scalp. He groaned and drew her bottom lip into his mouth, biting it, then soothing the sting with his tongue. Macy thought she would float away as pleasure sent her flying high. The world spun as he continued to kiss her.

With a growl, he pulled away. "We have to stop. You—I —" he broke off and growled again, swallowing hard before continuing. "We can't do this."

Macy sighed and let her hands slide to his chest. "No. Not here." She stood on her toes and nipped his bottom lip. "But don't for a second think I'm letting you blow me off when we get back to civilization. Not this time. You woke the beast, buddy, and she wants more." She stepped out of his arms and walked around him, entering the tent without looking back. A smile turned up the corners of her mouth. He wanted her and couldn't deny it. She just had to convince him they were worth the risk. That together, they were better than his unencumbered life.

Game on, Brady. Game on.

EIGHT

"I got one!" Hannah stood from her chair and reeled in her line. The end of the rod bobbed as she fought with the fish on the end. "Holy crap!"

"No fair," Jessie whined. "Everyone's caught one except me."

"Patience, grasshopper," Macy said. "Give it time." She smoothed the girl's blonde ponytail and smiled, then turned her attention to Hannah. Brady had the net ready to scoop up the fish once she got it near the shoreline. The fish splashed as it broke the surface, and he leaned forward, snatching it out of the water.

"That's a nice size perch, Hannah. Good job." Brady untangled the fish from the net.

She grinned up at him. "Thanks."

"A few more like that and we'll have a nice dinner tonight." He removed the hook from the fish's mouth and dropped it into the bucket next to his chair to swim along with the other two they caught.

Jessie reeled in her line and swung her arm back to cast it

out again. It only made it a few feet into the water, which was part of her problem.

Brady walked over and crouched beside her. "Let me see that pole."

She handed it over. He reeled in the line and stood up. "Let's get it out further. I think you'll have better luck." He swung his arm back and let it fly.

"Wow! That's like halfway into the lake."

He laughed. "Not quite, but there's probably some bigger fish out that way. Here." He handed her back her pole. "Reel it in nice and slow."

Macy smiled as she watched them, then cast her own line into the lake. She kept one eye on her line and another on Jessie. The young girl had her tongue stuck out and her brow furrowed as she stared at the water, willing a fish to take her bait. Her line went taut, and her face morphed into shock. "Oh! I got one!"

"Don't jerk the line," Brady said, stooping to help her. "Reel it in steadily."

She nodded. "It's a big one." Her rod dipped low over the water, and she pulled up on it.

"That's good. Keep reeling it in." He stood to grab the net and stepped to the water's edge.

Macy's line jerked, and she realized she had a fish as well. "I got another one. We're going to eat well tonight." She turned the reel, doing her best to watch Jessie, too. She wanted to see the girl's fish.

Brady leaned down, putting the net in the water to remove the fish splashing at the surface. "You got a bass." He removed it from the net and held it up. "That's a good one."

The little girl cheered. He took the hook out, then put the fish in the bucket.

Macy finished pulling in her fish. She caught the swinging line and grabbed the wriggling creature. "I got a bass, too.

Yum." She took it off the line and put it in the bucket with the others.

"Let's get a couple more, then call it a day. We'll take these back to camp and clean them up, then," Brady said.

"How do you clean a fish? Isn't it already clean since it's been in the water?" Jessie asked.

"Not clean as in wash, but clean as in remove the scales and guts and bones so we can eat it," he told her.

Her nose wrinkled. "Oh, yuck!"

"It's not that bad," Macy said, casting her line again. "And trust me, it's better than getting a scale or a little bone in your mouth when you're eating."

"For sure." Brady took Jessie's pole and cast her line into the water before handing it back.

They spent the next half hour fishing, catching three more fish. Jessie caught two of them. When they were done, Brady dispatched the fish and gutted them, then hung them off a stringer to make them easier to carry back to their campsite. Hannah and Jessie looked on in both fascination and disgust. Once he was done, and they had all their gear packed up, they set off on their hike back through the woods.

Macy started singing, trying to rein in some of Jessie's energy. The girl wanted to run ahead despite her encounter with the bear. She picked a song currently on the radio that the girls knew. Jessie slowed down to listen. To her surprise, Brady joined in, his rich bass a beautiful contrast to her mezzo-soprano.

After a few bars, both kids joined them. They sang a medley of songs on their way back to camp.

"I wish you'd brought your guitar," Macy told Brady as they walked into their campsite.

"Me too. But there wasn't room for it in the car."

"You play guitar?" Jessie said.

"Could you teach us?" Hannah asked. "I've always wanted to learn, but Mom said lessons were too expensive."

He shared a glance with Macy and shrugged. "Sure. We could meet in the evenings a couple times a week if it's okay with your mom."

"Yay!" Hannah hopped up and down, clapping her hands. "I'm excited."

He smiled. "Good. Carry that excitement over to cleaning this fish." He held up the stringer.

Her expression fell. She blew her blonde bangs out of her face and rolled her eyes. "Fine. What do we do?"

Macy laughed, patting Brady on the arm. "And with that, I will leave them with you. I'm going to start a fire so we can cook those babies once you get them cleaned."

He nodded. "Sounds good."

Macy walked toward the tent to stow her gear, removing the food wrappers and extra food to put back in the car. Brady gave her what he had in his pack and she put it in their garbage and food tubs in the vehicle, then took out the salt, pepper, and a bag of chips. She set them on the picnic table, then gathered some kindling. As she built the fire, she heard the occasional shout of disgust from one of her sisters, followed by Brady's deep laugh.

After she had the fire roaring, she found the tinfoil in their supplies and walked over to the plastic table where they were almost done cleaning the fish. She tore off several lengths of foil and laid them out, putting fish fillets on them. Hannah grabbed the salt and pepper and sprinkled each one, then Macy folded the foil over them. They laid them on the grate over the fire, then sat down to wait.

A cool wind blew through camp, making Macy shiver. She looked up at the sky, noting that it had grown overcast. She was surprised it wasn't raining already. The forecast showed rain all day, but they hadn't seen a drop yet. It had stayed in the higher elevations. But it looked like it was finally on its way.

The rush of water outside the tent woke Brady from a sound sleep. He yawned and touched the button on his watch to illuminate the dial. It was 3:20 a.m.

Pushing off his sleeping bag, he tugged on his jeans and pulled on his socks and boots. He grabbed his jacket and a flashlight and made his way to the front door of the tent. The zipper on the other room of the tent opened, and he glanced back. Macy stumbled out, bleary-eyed with her hair a mess. She shoved the mass away from her face and stared at him in the dark.

"What's going on? Why are you getting up?"

"I want to check the river. It's raining hard enough, we could see some flooding. Especially if this keeps up."

She frowned, her sleepy confusion cute. "Should I wake the kids and start packing?"

"Not yet. Let me check the water level. We should be high enough, but I'm not sure how much rain fell higher up the mountain already. We had a decent snow pack this year, so if it rained instead of snowed up there today, we could be in some trouble. I might use the sat phone and call home. See if I can get a weather report."

She smothered a yawn and nodded. "Okay."

He ducked out before he was tempted to tame all that glorious hair himself. Rain soaked him before he could get his jacket on. The icy water sluiced down the back of his neck and made him shiver. Damn, it wasn't far from turning to snow.

Shining the flashlight on the ground, he walked out of camp toward the river fifty yards away through the trees. He could hear the water rushing before he saw it. It flowed over the banks and through the trees nearby. The beam of his light bounced off the water as he watched it rush past. That was a lot of water. It must have dumped several inches up the mountain earlier.

He turned around and hurried back to camp. He needed to get a weather report.

Water dripped off him onto the tent floor as he stepped inside the door. Macy sat in a chair in the dark, waiting.

"Can you get the sat phone? It's in my bag." He pointed toward his room. "The river's high. Higher than what I would expect for the rain we've gotten here so far."

She nodded and got up, going into his room to dig through his bag, coming back out with the device.

He took it from her and powered it up, calling Seb, knowing he would be less alarmed about getting a middle of the night phone call than the others.

It rang four times before his brother's sleepy voice came on the line.

"Archer."

"Seb, it's Brady. I know it's the middle of the night, but can you go look at the weather radar for our area? It's pouring and the river's rising. Fast."

"Yeah, hang on." He heard rustling as Seb got out of bed. "Okay, let's see what's going on. It's raining here, but not too hard. I can hear the rain on your end. It sounds like it's coming down in buckets."

"It is."

Seb yawned. "Sorry. Um, radar shows heavy rain for your area. And it doesn't look like it'll let up anytime soon."

Great. "There a rainfall estimate anywhere?"

"Let me check the university website."

Brady took the towel Macy offered him and wiped some of the water from his hair and coat while he waited.

"Just shy of two inches so far just to your west. An inch for you. Rainfall rates are two inches an hour in parts of the system. It says total rainfall could exceed five inches."

His eyes widened. "Does it say anything about current totals at the higher elevations?"

"Let me see... Yeah, here we go. Above five thousand feet in your area, four inches have fallen since yesterday. There's still a big blob of rain over the mountains, too."

Brady gave an exasperated huff. "What the hell happened to scattered showers with the *chance* of locally heavier stuff."

Seb yawned again. "I guess the forecast changed. Are you good? Can I go back to bed?"

"Yeah, I'm good. We're coming home. Thanks. Bye." He hung up and looked at Macy. "We need to leave. The campsite is probably out of the normal floodplain, but I'm not sure it's far enough for this system. I'd rather not chance it." He relayed the forecast.

Her eyes widened. "I'll wake up the kids." She spun around.

Brady dropped the towel and spun around to go back outside and pull the car closer. He backed up near the door, then hurried over to the canopy and took down the table, then the canopy itself. Macy had the girls up, and the three of them were putting luggage in the back.

"All that's left is the tent," Macy said, ushering the kids into the backseat where it was dry.

"Let's hurry. We're still going to get soaked, but I'd like to avoid hypothermia. Leave the stakes in until last so it doesn't catch the wind as much."

She nodded and ran to the first tent pole, pulling it from its stay and yanking it free from the sleeve. Brady dashed to the other side and took out the other cross pole. They got the tent flat and all the poles out, then moved on to the tent stakes. As they picked up the corners to fold it, the wind kicked up, making it act like a sail. It jerked Macy off her feet, and she landed in the mud with a splat. He caught another of the lines to keep the tent from flying away and ran over to help her up.

"You okay?"

She nodded. "Yep. Let's wrestle this beast into the car and get out of here." She ran to the edge, standing on it so Brady could fold the material over. Between the two of them, they corralled the fabric flapping in the wind, getting it stuffed into its bag well enough they could get it in the car. Brady pushed the button to close the hatch and ran around to get in the driver's seat. He shook his head to get the water droplets out of his eyes.

"Let's go camping, she said. It'll be fun, she said." He swiped his face, then started the car.

Macy laughed. "Well, it was until someone pissed off Zeus."

He held up a hand. "Wasn't me."

"It was probably one of his kids. They're always testing Daddy's boundaries."

He laughed.

"You two are strange," Hannah said from the backseat with a giggle.

"No argument there," Macy said.

"Nope," Brady agreed. He steered the car onto the main road out of the campground. "Sorry, kids. Looks like our trip's been cut short." He glanced back to see them staring out their windows at the pouring rain.

"That's okay," Jessie said. "I miss my bed."

"It's only been one night," Hannah said.

"I know, but I have all those pillows and that fluffy comforter." She sighed.

"I should probably call Denise and let her know we're on our way home," Macy said to him.

He groaned. "I left the sat phone in the back of the car."

She sighed. "Never mind."

"Sorry."

"It's okay. I just wanted to give her a heads up. It's probably better this way, so she doesn't stay awake and worry. We won't wake her up much earlier than she normally gets up, anyway." She peered out at the rain. "Though, at the rate we're going, it'll be after her alarm goes off."

"Yeah. I can't see anything. How did they get this forecast so wrong?" He leaned forward, eyes locked on the road. The wipers were on as fast as they would go, and he was creeping, but could still barely see where they were going.

"It probably got hung up on the mountains and is just dumping on us."

"Well, whatever the reason, we need to get off this mountain and across that bridge at the base before the river floods over it. I think some of this excess water is snowmelt from higher elevations."

He steered them around the sharp curves, praying there weren't any other cars on the road. They were nearing the bottom when a low rumble caught his attention.

"What is that?" Macy said.

Small rocks pinged off the car. "Shit, it's a rock slide. Hang on." He punched the accelerator, hoping to get them clear of the debris path. Larger rocks smacked into the side of the vehicle and several softball-size ones bounced off the hood. Jessie and Hannah shrieked in the backseat and huddled together.

Without warning, the car slid, and Brady realized they were caught in the flow. The vehicle fishtailed, unable to get traction. Macy's window blew out as a baseball-size rock crashed through it. She screamed, the sound mixing with those from the kids, and she leaned toward him. He steered them into the skid, praying nothing larger hit the car and they could ride the slide down the embankment without rolling.

Macy clutched his arm as the car tipped. "Brady!"

"I know, Mace. I'm trying." He fought with the car, which wanted to roll over as they slid down the mountain. The flow pushed them into a tree, which stabilized them. The debris above them pushed them on top of the tree, taking all control out of Brady's hands. Fear gripped him, knowing he couldn't do anything to intervene. He covered Macy's hand with his and watched as they slid, praying harder than he ever had.

After a few seconds, which felt like minutes, they came to a stop. Small pebbles continued to ping off the car as the dirt settled. Hands shaking, Brady looked back. "You two okay?"

Still sobbing, they nodded.

He looked at Macy to ask her the same thing and noticed the sheen of blood on her face in the light from the dash. "Mace, you're bleeding."

She touched her forehead, wincing. "Yeah. It's from when the window blew out. I don't think it's that deep. We need to get out of here."

He leaned in to get a better look at her cut. Seeing she was right, and it wasn't serious, he pulled away and unbuckled his seat belt. "I can't get out my door. It's wedged against the tree we hit. Will yours open?"

She tried it, but it was stuck too.

"How about you, Jessie? Will yours open?" He knew Hannah's wouldn't because of the tree.

The little girl pulled on her door handle, pushing against the door. It cracked open, but wouldn't go more than a few inches.

"Okay, the window it is. Macy, you need to go out first."

She was already moving as he spoke, unbuckling her seat belt and pulling herself through the window to sit on the sill.

"There's a lot of water out here, Brady." She swung a leg out, then dropped down. He heard a splash as she touched down.

"Can't be helped. We can't stay here." He looked at the kids. "Jess, you're next. Climb up here, sweetie."

The little girl sniffed hard, hiccupping, and squeezed between the front seats. Brady helped her through the window, where Macy grabbed her and set her on the ground.

"Your turn, Hannah." He motioned the older girl forward.

She climbed into the front, and he helped her steady herself as she climbed out, taking Macy's hand as she swung her legs through the window.

Brady shut off the car and followed them out, having to do some fancy maneuvering to get his six-foot-seven frame through the window. Water covered his boots once he finally got his feet on the ground. He could hear it rushing just below them. "We're really close to the river."

"Yeah, and the water's getting higher," Macy said. "I can feel it creeping up my shoes the longer we stand here."

"Let's get some supplies from the back of the car and get the hell out of Dodge." He splashed around to the back, praying he could get the tailgate up. He wasn't above breaking the glass, though, to get inside. He pulled on the latch, and the door swung up. The bag with the tent poles rolled out. He left them there and took out the food and garbage tubs to get to their packs.

"You still have dry clothes and the refillable water bottles in your bag?" He glanced around the corner of the car at Macy. She nodded. He ducked back under the door, using it as a shield to load more food and emergency supplies into his pack. He added things to Macy's too, before closing the hatch and slogging back to her.

"I added more food and some water purification tablets."

She took it, putting it on. Brady strapped his on, then clicked the power button on his flashlight, shining it toward the sound of running water. The powerful light illuminated the rushing river through the rain only fifteen yards away.

"Hell." He stepped away from the car and shone the light up the embankment. A mess of uprooted trees and boulders met his gaze. He moved the beam side to side, looking down the bank, but in the dark, it was hard to tell where it was safe.

Macy stepped to his side. "Where do we go, Brady?"

He looked down at her, then back at the kids who huddled against the car, their faces blank with shock. "Up. I think we need to go up. But not that way." He motioned to the embankment where they'd slid down. "We need to walk along the bank and find a safer place to climb up, then hunker down somewhere until daylight. It's too dangerous to go far in the dark."

She nodded.

"Come on, girls." Brady motioned the kids to them. "We're going to walk that way for a bit and try to get back up to the road." He pointed up the riverbank. "Jessie, you stick with me, okay? Stay on my left, away from the river."

She hurried around to stand on his left, slipping her little hand into his. Determination hit Brady hard. He would not fail this child and would get her and her sister to safety.

They set off through the trees, using them to keep their footing as they walked across the soggy ground. More than once, Brady's feet slid in the muck. Jessie and Hannah had an easier time, their lighter weight keeping them from sinking.

"Should we try to make it back to camp?" Macy asked.

"No. It's too far away, and most of it's likely underwater now." The rain hadn't let up in the last hour they'd been on the road. "Our best chance is getting up to the road and flagging down another car. We can't be the only ones who left the campground."

"What about the sat phone?"

"I'll call if we can't flag someone down once we reach the

road. No one will be able to get to us until this rain lets up, anyway."

Hannah let out a shout of surprise. Brady swung the light in her direction and saw her sliding down the embankment toward the river.

"Grab a tree!"

She snagged a branch, halting her descent.

Brady looked at Jessie. "You stay here. I'm going to go get your sister." He saw Macy headed toward them and made sure Jessie had hold of a branch before walking down the steep slope, sliding from tree to tree.

"Are you okay?" he asked when he reached the girl.

She gave him a jerky nod. "Yeah. Do we have to go much further? My hands and feet are numb."

"I don't know. I've been looking for an overhang. If we can find one, we'll park ourselves under it until morning. Give me your hand."

She held out her hand. It was ice cold in his. He pulled her away from the tree and wrapped an arm around her waist, using his free hand to pull them up the embankment tree by tree. Mud caked his boots by the time he reached Macy.

Without a word, she took Jessie's hand, and they set off across the slope once more, taking care to hold on to branches as they moved so no one slid downhill again.

"Up there." Brady's light bounced off some rocks. They jutted out over the slope, leaving an overhang.

"Oh, thank God," Hannah said, scurrying toward the outcropping.

They scrambled over the ground, eager to be out of the rain. Once under it, both kids sank down, huddling together against the rock. The area was large enough that there was a decent dry spot underneath. He and Macy unstrapped their packs and set them down. He opened his, looking for the stash of hand warmers he packed.

"Everyone take your boots off. We need to get our feet warm and dry."

"I can't get mine untied," Hannah said, tears making her voice thick. "My fingers are too numb."

"I've got it, honey," Macy said, moving to the girl's feet. "You just relax, okay?"

Hannah nodded and sniffed.

Brady found the warmers and went to sit down with them. He cracked the packets and held them out to Macy. "Have them put these between their coats and their clothes. Under their arms and on their bellies."

She took them as he cracked them, helping the girls get them situated, then finished removing Hannah's boots and socks. She fished the dry socks from her wet bag in her pack and slid them over the girl's feet, rolling up her wet pant legs to keep the socks dry, before moving to Jessie and helping her do the same.

Brady gave them each a protein bar. "Eat. It'll help warm you up."

They unwrapped the bars while he and Macy took off their shoes, changing into dry socks. They put warmers under their coats as well. He gave her a bar and took one for himself, moving back to lean against the rock face. She scooted up next to him. Jessie sat in her lap while Hannah tucked herself against Macy's side.

"I want to go home," Jessie said.

Macy kissed the top of her head. "I know you do. And we will. But we need to stay here for now. It's too dangerous to keep going at the moment." She patted the girl on the back. "Try to get some sleep."

The little girl snuggled deeper into Macy's chest. Hannah wrapped her arm around Macy's, laying her head on her shoulder.

Brady's mind worked overtime as he weighed the gravity

of their situation. If they could stay warm tonight—and the rain quit—they could hike up to the road in the morning and find help.

Macy sagged against him. He lifted an arm and wrapped it around her, pulling her and the girls closer, then rested his head against the rocks behind him. Rain continued to pound down around them, making it feel like they were the only people in the world. In this corner of it, they were. He clutched Macy a little closer at that thought.

Nine

The chirp of the birds drew Macy awake. Her eyes fluttered open, and she squinted against the bright morning light. It was still overcast, but the rain had stopped. She shifted to sit up straight, her back and knees protesting the hard ground as well as being in the same position for so long.

Brady took a deep breath, waking up. He yawned and looked at her.

"Morning." His low voice was even lower from sleep.

"Morning." She shifted Jessie, sliding the girl to the ground between them. She mumbled, but didn't wake up. Hannah woke, looking at her through bleary eyes.

"You can lie back down with your sister for a bit, if you want. I have to pee." Macy scooted forward to put her shoes on, then stand. Hannah sank down to curl up with Jessie.

"You pack any toilet paper when you threw stuff in your bag?" She looked down at Brady.

He yawned again and got to his feet. "Yeah. There's a roll in yours too."

"Awesome." She picked up her pack and walked out from under the overhang. This was seriously going to suck. Not only did she hate peeing in the woods, but there was a bite to the air. Her ass was going to freeze.

She found a thick copse of young trees to do her business behind, using a stick to dig a hole and bury her toilet paper once she was done. Ass numb both from the cold and from sitting on the hard ground for hours, she walked back to the overhang.

Both kids were awake now and needed to use the restroom. She took them to her stand of trees and coached them through the process. Once they both went, they went back to their rocky camp, where Brady had a map and compass out.

"Where are we?" Macy asked, standing next to him to look at the map.

He pointed to a spot. The river ran along one side, the mountain range on the other.

"How do we get out of here?"

He folded the map to put it away. "We find the road. If we can't flag down a car, I'll call Seb." He looked at the kids. "You two ready to go?"

They nodded and stood.

"Let's go. Watch your footing. The ground is still soggy."

Picking their way over the uneven, muddy ground, they used the trees again to help them keep their footing. The hillside grew steeper the further they walked. Macy stopped to rest against a tree. "It gets much steeper and we're going to have to turn back."

He eyed the slope above them. Macy glanced up. It went close to vertical the closer it was to the road. There was no way they could climb seventy feet up a cliff with no safety gear. She looked down. They'd only come up about thirty feet from the riverbank, unable to rise higher because of the angle. She could see the water rushing below. The first threads of panic crept in as the feeling of being trapped hit her. Taking a deep breath, she looked away from the river to focus on Brady. His calm demeanor helped keep her from losing it.

"You three stay here. I'm going to walk ahead a bit and see if it levels out any."

Macy nodded. "Come on, girls. Let's sit with our backs to some trees, so we don't slide down the hill, and give our legs a break." They made their way to her, the three of them huddling above a small cluster of trees as Brady took off through the foliage.

"Can I have another protein bar?" Jessie asked. "I'm hungry."

"How about some trail mix?" They needed to ration their high protein food, just in case.

"Okay."

Macy pulled her pack off and dug inside. "Hannah, do you want some?"

"Sure."

She handed both girls a packet of trail mix and their water bottles. Not hungry, Macy skipped the food, but took a drink.

"How long do you think we'll be stuck out here?" Hannah asked.

"I'm not sure. Hopefully, only a few more hours. Once we get up to the road, it'll just be a matter of time until we come across a car or Brady gets a hold of Sebastian." It was getting up there in the first place that was going to be the problem, though. She was beginning to think they should just wait here and call Seb to send in a rescue team.

"I'm cold," Jessie said.

Macy pulled the girl into her lap and wrapped her arms around her. "We get moving again and you'll warm up." She hoped Brady came back soon. Sitting still was making her cold, too.

They huddled together to stay warm while they waited, chatting about what they were going to do once they got home. Number one on all their lists was a hot bath. Macy couldn't wait to sink into her tub. She'd fill it full of bubbles, turn on some music and drink a big glass of wine. It sounded heavenly.

When Brady returned fifteen minutes later, they had a whole plan for when they returned to civilization.

"Well? Does it get any better?"

"A little. The slope flattens enough a few minutes away that we should be able to climb up to the road."

Macy lifted Jessie off her lap. "Let's go, then. I'm ready for my bubble bath."

"What?" He frowned at her.

The kids giggled.

"Inside joke," she told him. "Lead the way, so we can go home."

He shook his head, but turned to keep walking. They followed him, doing their best to stay upright. As she watched her footing, she heard a snap. Jessie shrieked. Macy whirled to see the girl tumble sideways down the hill as the branch she held broke off.

"Jessie!" She took two steps toward the girl, but Brady flew past her, sidestepping down the hill after the child.

"Hannah, stay where you are," Macy said. She pointed to a tree. "Hang on and stay put." She took off down the slope after Brady. Jessie still tumbled down. How the girl didn't slam into a tree, Macy didn't know. As she slid down through the mud and leaves, she watched in horror as Jessie rolled into the river, her little body getting swallowed by the rushing torrent. Hannah screamed.

"No!" Brady's shout echoed over the hillside.

The girl's head popped above the water downstream.

"There!" Macy pointed.

"I see her." He took off down the bank, shedding his pack and his coat.

Macy's eyes widened. *Dear God. He was going in after her.*

The icy water stole Brady's breath as he dove into the river after Jessie. He took a moment to gather himself, letting the water carry him. Once he could breathe without gasping, he started swimming, propelling himself toward the girl. She kept going under as the current pulled her downstream. Just before he reached her, she disappeared and didn't come back up. He threw everything he had into his last few strokes, then dove beneath the surface, feeling around desperately for the girl.

His hand moved through a cloud of hair. Relief shot through him. He kicked harder to reach further down and felt for her collar. Finding it, he curled his fingers around it and tugged, then shot to the surface. He pulled in a deep breath. Jessie coughed and wretched, throwing up river water. He tucked her into a rescue carry and sidestroked toward the bank closest to them, which was opposite from where they went in. His powerful legs fought the current, taking them closer to safety. When his heel hit the bottom, he pushed off and stood, lifting Jessie into his arms as he trudged through the knee-deep water to the bank.

Free from the river, he laid the girl in the mud. She sobbed through bouts of heavy coughing, her lungs expelling the water she inhaled.

"You're okay." He stroked her forehead, then hugged her to his chest, tears welling in his eyes as it hit him how close she came to drowning. "You're safe now. You're okay." He murmured to her until she calmed down some.

"Does anything hurt?" He pulled away to look at her.

She held up her left arm. "My wrist." Brady could see some bruising and swelling on the thumb side. "And my head." She pointed to her forehead with her other hand. A scrape and a knot the size of a quarter marred an area near her hairline.

Her lip wobbled, signaling to him she was ready to break into tears again. He smiled down at her. "Is that all? After that fall you took? I've done worse falling off my horse."

The small smile Brady was aiming to get spread over her face.

"Brady!"

He looked up at Macy's shout. She and Hannah stood across the river.

"Is she okay?"

"Yeah. We're good."

"What do we do now?" She gestured to the river between them.

"Get the sat phone out of my pack and call Seb."

She crouched down, opening his bag, which she'd picked up on her dash down the riverbank, and dug through it, finding the phone.

"No. No, no, no!"

"What? What's wrong?"

"It won't turn on. It must have gotten wet."

He groaned and pinched the bridge of his nose. Okay, new plan. He ran the map he looked at earlier through his head, trying to decide where to go. Jessie would never make it back across the river. On this side, though, they had a clear shot out of the river valley to the next town. He stood, looking upstream and down. It narrowed some to his left.

"You guys need to cross."

"What?"

Even from a distance, he could see the perplexed look on her face.

"There are a couple ropes in my pack and the river narrows down there. If we tie one of them off on both sides of the river, you two can hang on to it and cross. It's our only option unless we split up, and I don't want to do that."

"Maybe Hannah and I could make it up the embankment to the road. You said it flattened some."

"Yeah, but not much. After what happened, I'm not inclined to have you two risk that slope again without climbing gear. Get the rope and meet us down there." He pointed downstream. "We have a clear shot to town from this side of the river."

Her shoulders dropped, but she nodded.

Brady turned to Jessie, stooping to pick her up. She wrapped her good arm around his neck, shivering. He quickened his pace. The faster he could get her sisters across the river, the faster he could start a fire and get them all warm.

He found the spot where it would be the easiest for them to cross and set Jessie down well away from the water.

"How am I supposed to get this rope to you?" Macy said.

"Tie it around a rock and throw it. Just pick one you know you can throw that far."

She enlisted Hannah to help her find a suitable rock.

"I'm really glad you taught me how to tie a decent knot." She looped the rope around the rock, securing it.

He was, too. This wouldn't work if the rock slipped free of the rope. The nylon rope was too light to carry very far.

"Okay. I think I'm ready."

"Tie the other end to a strong tree."

She hurried up the bank, finding a suitable tree trunk and doing as he said.

"Fire away, babe."

He could see her muttering to herself as she pulled her arm back, and he couldn't help the twitch of his lips. She was probably telling him not to call her babe.

She let the rock fly, the rope stringing out behind it. It splashed into the water two feet from the bank. He hurried forward to grab it before the current took it, walking up the bank into the trees to tie it up. Pulling it taut, he secured it, then went back to the riverbank. "Okay, it's secure. Hannah, you come first. Macy will be right behind you."

The girl edged toward the water, wearing Macy's backpack. Macy, wearing his pack and jacket, gave her an encouraging squeeze on her shoulder and said something to her. He watched her take a deep breath and close her eyes a moment before wading into the water and grabbing the rope.

"Wrap an arm around it," he told her. "In case your hands go numb." The water was chilly from the snow melt flowing into it.

She did as he said, wrapping it around her arm, pulling herself forward with the other. He shook his head in awe as she drew closer. The James sisters were some of the toughest kids he knew.

He waded into the water as far as he dared and reached out to help her to shore. She sloshed past him to fall to her knees on the bank, exhausted. He made sure she was far enough away from the river's edge, then turned back to help Macy. When she was close enough, she took his outstretched hand, and he pulled her toward him. She clung to him, catching her breath.

"You okay?" He pulled back to see her face.

She nodded. "Yeah." She stepped out of his arms and headed for Jessie, dropping down in front of the girl.

"Are you all right?"

Jessie nodded, her lip wobbling again. "I'm okay."

Tears coursed down Macy's cheeks. "I'm so glad." She tugged the girl into her arms for a hug.

Brady cleared his throat, emotion clogging it. "She probably broke her wrist. We need to splint it and find some dry firewood to start a fire."

Macy sniffed and looked back at him. "Aren't there some

caves on this side of the river? I think I remember reading something about that when Deck and I planned this trip. We talked about trying to find them, but decided it would be too difficult to ford the river." She rolled her eyes. "Little did we know..."

He flashed a smile at her. "Yeah. And I think you're right. Let's see if we can find one. Get the map out again." He was grateful for the wet bags they carried. He just wished he'd put the sat phone in one. Buried beneath all the other stuff in his pack, he didn't think it would get wet enough to kill it. He'd been wrong, and he hoped it didn't cost them their lives.

She took off his pack and dug out the wet bag, finding the map and handing it to him. He accepted it with numb fingers, unfolding it to look for their location.

Hannah walked over to look, bouncing on the balls of her feet to stay warm. "The map shows you where the caves are?"

"It shows me changes in elevation." He traced the lines with his finger, showing her what he meant. "The caves we want will be near the base of the hills." He looked up, scanning the woods before handing the map back to Macy. "Okay. Let's get Jessie's wrist splinted, then we'll head that way." He nodded ahead of them, deeper into the forest.

"Is there a splint in the first aid kit?" Macy asked.

"Not for a wrist. There's an ace bandage, though. Can you get that out while I find some sticks?"

She nodded. He walked several feet away, looking at the ground. Hannah came with him. He picked up a suitable one and showed it to her. "We need several like this."

"Okay."

Between the two of them, they found what they needed. Brady took the twigs and bandage and kneeled next to Jessie, who sat propped against a tree trunk. He lifted her arm and she winced.

"I'm sorry, sweetie. Once I get it wrapped, it'll feel better."

She nodded, determination in her brown eyes. "I know. I can handle it."

He smiled at her. "I know you can. You're a tough cookie."

Macy stooped on her other side, holding the sticks in place while he wrapped the girl's hand and arm. He secured the bandage, then helped the girl to her feet, nudging her toward the woods.

"Let's find us a cave."

TEN

Macy's feet were numb. And her hands. Her legs felt like popsicles, the fabric of her insulated leggings clinging like wet plastic wrap.

She glanced at Hannah, who walked next to her. Dark circles colored the skin under her eyes, her face pale, but she didn't complain. Just trudged forward as they continued to look for a place to take shelter.

Jessie had long ago given up on walking. Brady now carried her. There were lines of fatigue etched around his eyes as he put one foot after another, moving forward.

They'd climbed out of the river valley and over some low hills, never leaving the thick forest. In the distance, she could see the ground rise sharply. The idea they might soon find a cave spurred her on, and she quickened her pace. In minutes, they were standing at the base of another cliff.

"Great. How do we get past that?" Hannah said.

"We don't. We walk along it until we find a path to the top or a cave." Brady looked at Macy. "Can I see that map again?"

She shrugged off her pack and dug out the map.

He set Jessie on her feet and took it. Glancing over it, he traced the river. "I think we're here." He pointed to a spot.

"Okay. We're in the right place, then. This is the area with the cave system."

He looked both directions, then down at the map. "I don't know where they'd be, but we need to go that way." He pointed to his right. "Town's that way and the terrain flattens." He folded up the map and handed it back to her.

She stowed it in the wet bag and shouldered the pack again. He picked up Jessie, and they set off parallel to the cliff. Macy scanned the rock face, looking for any sign of an entrance into the wall.

"There!" Hannah pointed up. "What's that?"

They stopped to look where she pointed.

"It does look like a cave entrance," Brady said. "But I don't know if we can get up there. It's pretty high."

"I think we can climb it. It's not that far," Macy said. "Twenty feet? Thirty?" Her eyes traveled over the rocks. "And I see a decent climbing path with lots of hand and footholds." She looked at him. "Do you think you can make it, holding her?" She gestured to Jessie.

He tipped his head and looked at the girl. "You think you can cling to my back like a monkey with your good arm?"

She nodded. "It means we can build a fire if we get up there, right?"

"Hopefully, yes."

"Let's do it."

Brady looked at the rock face. "Okay. Let's give it a shot. Macy, you go first. It'll be easier for you to pick out areas of loose rock, so I can avoid them. Hannah, you follow her and step where she steps."

The girl nodded.

Macy spun around and stared at the cliff, studying it a moment before taking her first steps up the side. It had quite a few natural ledges, making it feel more like a strange staircase than a cliff. About half way up, she looked back and motioned Hannah to join her. The girl took a breath to steady her nerves, then stepped onto the rock face.

Reaching the cave entrance, Macy peered inside. Blackness greeted her.

"Will it work?" Hannah pulled herself into the cave mouth.

"I think so."

Brady cursed, and Macy heard a cascade of small rocks bounce down to the forest floor. She turned and looked down. He was a few feet from the ledge, resting against the wall, and reassuring Jessie they were okay.

"You all right?"

He looked up, nodding. "Yeah. My foot slid." He started climbing again, reaching her in moments.

Macy grabbed hold of Jessie's good arm and helped her off his back, pulling her into the cave as Brady made it onto the ledge. He stood, but had to stoop to avoid the low ceiling.

"Have you gone deeper yet?"

She shook her head. "No. I wanted to make sure we all made it first."

"Well, no time like the present. Where are the flashlights?"

Macy and Hannah took off their packs, resting them against the cave wall, and dug through them, locating the lights.

"You two stay here," Brady said to the kids. "Take off your wet clothes while you wait and put on the dry items from the wet bag. If we're not back by the time you finish, start gathering leaves, grass, and small twigs for kindling. There's probably plenty that's been blown into the cave."

Hannah nodded and walked over to her sister. "Come on, Jessie. I'll help you get your stuff off."

Macy flipped on her light. "You ready?"

"Yep." He turned on his flashlight and stepped deeper into the cave. "My shoulders and neck are going to hate me later." He pointed his light at the low ceiling, then back in front of him.

"If my hands ever unfreeze, I'll rub them for you."

"Let's see what's in here, then. You aren't the only one who wants to thaw out."

They moved further into the cave, finding that it went back much further than they expected. They saw evidence of small mammal activity, but no large predators. Fifty yards in, it narrowed to the point they would have to crawl if they wanted to look deeper.

"I think I'm satisfied nothing's going to come eat us." Macy spun around. "Let's build a fire. I need to get out of these pants."

He coughed. Macy blushed as she realized how that sounded. She kept the light trained on the ground and her eyes on the light, avoiding his gaze, and kept walking. On the way back to the mouth of the cave, they collected small limbs and other items to make a fire. They added it to the pile the kids started.

Brady pushed it closer to the entrance and rearranged it some, then lit it with the matches he pulled from the survival kit in his pack. "Hopefully, the smoke won't drift inside too much."

The girls scooted closer, their backs to the cave as they huddled together. Macy walked over to her backpack to find her dry clothes. "I'm going to change."

"Me too." He dug into his own pack, pulling out a clean shirt and pants.

Macy eyed him, then the dark depths of the cave, trying to decide if she should muster up the energy to change in private. It wasn't like he hadn't already seen her naked, though, and in the end, fatigue won out. She took off her sodden coat and whipped her shirt over her head. Brady's face was priceless. Those deep, dark eyes went wide, the whites showing all the way around. His mouth parted ever so slightly.

He let out a strangled moan and turned around. "Warn a guy next time, would you?" His movements jerky, he drew his shirt over his head.

It was Macy's turn to stare. Muscles rippled in his broad back. Tattoos wound around his arms and decorated his shoulder blades.

Turn around! She wanted to see all of his powerful torso.

But he kept his back to her. She didn't complain, though. As she tried to make her muscles work so she could dress, he unfastened his pants and peeled them down his thick thighs. His wet boxer-briefs clung to his backside. He had the most magnificent ass. The tight muscles shifted under the damp fabric as he stood first on one foot, then the other to take off his pants.

Macy's mouth ran dry, all the moisture in her body flooding south. She wasn't so cold anymore.

He glanced back, growing still as he realized she hadn't moved. Heat licked his eyes in answer to what she was sure shone in hers.

The wind shifted, blowing into the cave, sending chilly, smoky air at them. Goosebumps erupted over her arms and a shiver went down her spine, motivating her to stop staring and put on her shirt. She drew the soft cotton over her head and pushed her arms into the sleeves. Her pants came off next, and she quickly drew on a dry pair. Brady dressed while she did. Barefoot, they walked over to the fire with their wet clothes. Macy picked up Jessie's and Hannah's and laid them out next to hers to dry, then sat down on the hard ground and pulled on a pair of socks. Brady put their boots as close to the fire as he dared, then grabbed his pack before sitting next to her. He covered his own feet in thick wool socks, then dug into his bag, withdrawing protein bars and trail mix.

Jessie made a face as she took the food. "I don't like these things. I want a cheeseburger."

"Me too," Brady said. "But we need to keep up our strength." He took the bar and tore open the package, then handed it back to her.

Nose wrinkled, she took a bite.

"What do we do now?" Hannah asked.

"Well, we're going to stay here for the night. Dry out, warm up. Tomorrow, I'm going to climb to the top of the ridge and see what I can see. We need to head toward town, but I don't know what's flooded, and the last thing we need is to end up back in the water."

"So, for now we just sit here?"

He nodded.

Her shoulders fell.

"How about we play a game?" Macy said, hoping to perk her up.

"What kind of game?"

Macy thought. "The one where you have to think of something that starts with the last letter of the previous word? So, if we start with the letter A and I say autumn, you have to say something that starts with the letter N."

She bit her lip. "Okay. Nice."

Macy looked at Jessie.

"Um, eye."

Everyone looked at Brady.

"Oh, it's my turn? Right. Um, Elbert."

That made the kids giggle. Macy flexed her fingers as she smiled, some of the feeling coming back. She could think of worse places to be stuck and worse people to be stuck with. If it weren't for their situation, it would just be another night at camp.

Brady woke to the feel of a warm weight on his chest. In the pre-dawn light, he could make out Macy's head rising and falling with every breath he took. He reached a hand up, tangling his fingers in her silky hair, the coppery strands flowing over his hand in cool waves. An ache spread in his chest. He wanted this woman in the worst way. But he knew if they went down that road again, she wouldn't let things stay casual. He wasn't sure he could do more, no matter how much she tempted him. Not after all the pain his ex-wife caused him. But damn, he wanted her anyway. Waking up next to her was nice. More so than he imagined.

Macy stirred, her pretty blue eyes fluttering open. She yawned and stretched, sitting up. "Sorry. I didn't mean to use you as a pillow." She kept her voice low. The kids were still sleeping.

"It's okay. We kept each other warm."

She nodded. He glanced at their now defunct fire.

"Speaking of, we should get that going again." He got to his feet, needing some space, and began gathering more of the small branches they scavenged yesterday to lay them over the ashes. Macy brought him the matches, and he lit the fire. It crackled to life, bringing some warmth back to the cave.

He found his boots and stuffed his feet into them. "I'm going to climb up to the top of this cliff and see what we're facing."

"What? Now? The sun's barely up."

"I know, but I'd like us to keep moving. Seb's probably looking for us, but our best chance is still hiking out of here."

Her mouth flattened. "Okay. But be careful. There's a lot of loose stone."

He nodded. "I will. Come running if you hear a bunch of rocks falling."

She smacked his shoulder. "Not funny!"

"Sorry, I couldn't resist." He smiled and moved over to his pack, finding his binoculars and the other rope he packed. Once he reached the top of the cliff, he would find a place to tie it off to help him get back down as well as help the kids and Macy climb up.

"I'll be back soon." He slung the rope over his neck and shoulder, then ducked out and took his first steps up the rock face.

Like the climb to the cave, there were a series of narrow ledges jutting out of the wall. Taking slow, methodical steps, he climbed up from ledge to ledge until he made it the forty feet to the top. From there, he was able to scrabble up the steep slope to the ridgeline.

Wind whipped around him, ruffling his hair and chapping his cheeks as he stared out over the valley. The river was well out of its banks, making a trek through the flatter ground impossible. He lifted the binoculars, scanning the mountainside and saw several recent landslides; he was sure there were more he couldn't see.

In the distance, the floodwaters disappeared around a bend between two mountains. The town he saw on the map was on the other side of those hills. They were going to have to trek north and stick to the slope to get around the flooding. It would be at least one more night before they got out of here, unless Seb found them first.

It was not what he wanted to see, but also not unexpected. He looked back the way they came, seeing glimpses of the road above the trees. More landslides obscured sections of the pavement. He was glad they came this way. No one was traversing that road anytime soon.

Done assessing their route out of the mountains, he turned around and made his way back to the cave. He found a decent tree close to the edge and tied the rope around it, then climbed down, sending small pebbles skittering to the ground.

Macy poked her head out of the cave. "You okay?"

"Yeah. Just some loose stone." He continued his backward walk down the rock face until he made it to the cave.

"What did you find?" She stepped back as he came inside.

"Nothing unexpected. We've got another night out here, though. We have to stick to the slopes. There's too much flooding in the valley to take a direct route through to the next town. We need to get moving, too. It looks like it could rain again."

Her face pulled in a frown. "Okay. I'll go get the kids and tell them we're leaving."

He glanced around, noting they were nowhere to be seen. "Where are they, anyway?"

"They wanted to explore the cave. They got bored playing the alphabet game." She turned. "I'll go get them."

As she wandered away, he kneeled next to his pack and stowed his binoculars, then removed a power bar. He was going to be sick of the things as much as Jessie was by the time they reached civilization.

"Brady!"

He rose, staring into the darkness at the sound of Macy calling his name.

"Macy?"

"Get down here!"

He took off at a run, slowed by his need to hunch. "What's wrong?" he asked as he closed in on her at the back of the cave. He looked around the area illuminated by her light. "Where are the kids?"

She pointed the flashlight at the narrow opening in the wall. "In there."

"Shit, are they stuck?" He walked closer. That was just what they needed. He had no idea how he was going to bust two kids out of a space he couldn't fit into and without any tools.

"We're not stuck," Hannah said.

Brady peered inside. It opened up again after twenty feet or so. The girls huddled together over something on the ground. "What are you doing back there?"

"We found something," Jessie said. There was a wobble in her voice, making the hair on the back of Brady's neck stand on end.

"What did you find?"

"A body," Hannah said.

Dumbstruck, he looked at Macy. She shrugged.

"I couldn't believe it either, but Hannah took a picture and showed it to me. There's a skeleton back there."

"Well, hell." He sighed. "Okay. There's nothing we can do about it now. We need to get ourselves to safety, then we can tell Seb and he can send a team in here." He looked back into the crevice. "Hannah, take a bunch of pictures of the area back there. Not just of the body, but all around, then you two come out."

"Okay."

He heard the beep of the camera and the shutter close as she did what he asked.

"Who do you think it is?" Macy asked.

"I have no clue. If it's a skeleton, whoever it is has been there a long time. Could be a hiker that got lost, or someone who decided this cave was home and then later died here. We'll get the images to Seb. Hopefully, he can get someone in there to retrieve the remains and figure out who it is."

"Whoever it is had to be small. Hannah barely fit. I could probably get in there, but I'd have to army crawl and pray my boobs weren't too big."

His eyes dropped to her chest, unbidden, for a fleeting

second. It was long enough for her to notice, though. When his eyes met hers, a slow, naughty smile spread over her face.

He cleared his throat, feeling the fire in his face, and looked into the crevice. Jessie's small body wiggled through with ease, even with her busted wrist. He helped her out, setting her on her feet, then turned to help her sister through the opening.

Once on her feet, she handed him the camera. "I spun a full three-sixty."

Brady touched the button to look at the images she took. Macy squeezed in beside him as he scrolled through. When they got to the skeleton, he cursed.

"You're right, he or she is small. It looks like a young teenager or maybe a tiny female, though the clothing looks male." He frowned and powered off the camera, his mind working as he tried to remember hearing about any missing kids or women in the last few years. Nothing came to mind. He prayed this wasn't more of the child trafficking ring his brother busted up. "Come on. Let's get out of here. The sooner we get back to town, the sooner we're safe and can get some answers."

Because he was ninety-nine percent certain that person back there hadn't chosen to live out his or her days in this cave.

Eleven

"We're going to have to find a stream and fill up our bottles," Brady said a few hours later, stopping next to Macy as she drank the last of her water.

"I was just thinking the same thing." They stopped a few minutes ago to take a quick break and had now used the last of their water.

"The trouble will be finding one not full of silt from the runoff."

"What are you thinking?" She studied him as he studied the mountain around them.

"That I need to get higher."

Macy glanced around. "Again? Where?" Her eyes widened as she took in his meaning. "You're going to climb a tree? You'll never get high enough to see much. The foliage is too dense and you're too heavy. The only one of us who could is Jessie, and she can't climb with her wrist."

He frowned. "All right. Let's head to the ridge." He pointed up. Macy could just make out the top of the hill from where they stood. It was up another steep slope.

"My legs hate you."

"I'll massage them for you later." His face grew bright red as soon as the words left his mouth.

Macy laughed. "I'm going to hold you to that." She walked past him, making sure to put some extra sway in her hips. She told the girls where they were going and ushered them ahead of her.

She glanced back. Brady's eyes were on her ass. She turned around to hide her smile.

Higher and higher they climbed. Macy's thighs burned by the time they broke free of the trees to stand at the top.

"Oh! I see the town!" Hannah pointed to the distance, where miles away rooftops dotted the landscape. "We can get there by nighttime."

Macy patted her shoulder. "Distance out here is deceiving. That's at least ten miles."

Her shoulders fell. "Really?"

"Yeah."

"But there's a stream, so we won't get dehydrated at least." Brady pointed down the hill.

"Where? I don't see a stream," Hannah said.

"Look at the trees. See the ones down there that look like someone drew a line between them?"

"Over there?" She pointed.

He nodded. "Yep. Come on. Let's get down there. We need to think about shelter for the night too. I don't think the rain is going to hold off much longer."

Jessie pouted. "Does that mean we have to eat more protein bars?"

He looked at Macy. She just stared back, knowing the answer.

"I'm afraid so, munchkin, unless I can catch something." He took her water bottle and put it in his pack, then motioned her to start walking.

"What would you catch? Fish?"

"Probably not. I'm not very good at hand-fishing. I might be able to trap a squirrel or a rabbit, though."

She wrinkled her nose. "I don't want to eat that. The protein bars are fine."

He chuckled. "Rabbit's not bad. Squirrel isn't my favorite, though."

The cry of an eagle overhead drew their attention. Macy looked up to see the enormous bird swoop past, riding an air current down the mountain to circle over the treetops.

"Wow! That was cool! They're ginormous."

Macy giggled. "Yes, they are. How about we see what else we can spot? Just watch your footing, though. We don't want anyone to fall."

As they made their way down the ridge, the girls pointed out different animals and plants they saw. Macy and Brady played along, but kept an eye on the sky. It was growing darker by the minute.

An icy wind whipped through the trees, and the first wet flakes of snow started to fall. She edged closer to Brady. "Was it supposed to do this?" She pointed at the snowflakes falling around them.

His mouth flattened. "No, but we're at a higher elevation, and I didn't look at the forecast for up here. Regardless, we're never going camping in April again."

"Agreed. Maybe it'll change to rain. Though, I'm not sure that's any better."

"No. It could cause more landslides. Let's pick up the pace. We need to fill our bottles and find shelter."

Not wanting to alarm the kids, Macy caught up with Hannah, walking faster, encouraging the girl to stay close without telling her to move more quickly. Brady scooped Jessie up and set her on his shoulders. They picked their way down the hillside at a steady pace, the snow falling faster. By the time they reached the stream, a dusting covered the ground.

"Can we build a snowman?" Jessie asked.

"Maybe after we find shelter, okay? We don't want to get caught out in the cold in the dark."

"Will we be able to find another cave?" Hannah asked. "What happens if we can't?"

"I'll build us a lean-to if we don't find something soon. It won't be as cozy as a cave, but it'll keep the rain and snow off of us."

"How do you build a lean-to?"

Brady looked up, laughing, as Jessie dipped her head down to look into his eyes. "You prop or tie together some branches against a tree, then cover it with pine boughs."

"Oh." She sat up. "Neat."

"It's very neat. And knowing how to build one is a useful skill to have. You two are getting a crash course in survival."

At the edge of the stream, Macy took off her backpack and found the water purification tablets and her bottle. The water was high, but looked fairly clear. She knew, though, there could still be parasites and bacteria lurking.

Brady set Jessie on the ground and removed his and the girls' water bottles from his bag. He took Macy's, then filled them all. She dropped the requisite number of tablets in each bottle before recapping them and swirling the water.

"How long do we have to wait before we can drink it?" Hannah asked, watching the process with a keen eye.

"At least thirty minutes," Brady replied. "Let's keep moving. If we haven't found a shelter in an hour, we'll make one."

They splashed through the shallow stream to continue their trek. The snowfall grew heavier, and after a half hour, Brady signaled them to stop. There was now an inch on the ground, and the wind had kicked up considerably.

"We need to build that shelter. Girls, go find as many long, thin branches as you can carry. But stay within sight of me or Macy at all times, okay?"

They nodded and took off.

"What do you want me to do?" Macy asked.

"Find some larger branches for the basic structure and pile them near those trees." He pointed to a cluster a few feet away. "I'm going to start cutting off pine boughs for the roof."

Macy assessed the surrounding forest, noting several downed branches and small trees that would be suitable. She walked to the nearest one and dragged it to the spot Brady indicated. Within a few minutes, they had a decent pile to start their shelter with.

A mass of pine boughs landed to her left as Brady dumped them on the ground.

"Here." He held out his knife. "Cut some more boughs for our roof. I'll start lashing the branches together."

Macy took the blade and headed for the closest pine tree, lopping off the low, smaller branches covered in pine needles.

The snow continued to fall while they worked. Macy hoped they could get a fire going once they finished the shelter. With the wind the way it was and the snow, she wasn't sure they could get one to light.

While she continued to gather pine boughs, the girls held branches in place as Brady tied them together into a semblance of a structure. He wove the smaller branches through the larger ones to strengthen it. Hannah caught on to what he was doing and started on the other side.

"Girls, I need you to go find as much dead wood as you can. It can be wet, but make sure it's not a recent fall. We need to start a fire," Brady said.

Hannah nodded and ran back into the trees. Jessie followed at a slower pace. Macy eyed her, concerned. The girl never did anything at less than full speed.

"We need to get this shelter up and a fire going. Now. Jessie's hurting."

"I noticed that too. She's been through the ringer. Let's get started on the pine boughs. Hopefully, we cut enough."

"Well, there's always more." Macy gestured around them.

"No doubt." He walked over to the pile they'd made and picked up a handful of the branches. He layered them over the top of the shelter, stopping the wet snow from collecting inside the partial structure.

Once the top was covered, he started on the sides. He kneeled at the base of the lean-to and began adding boughs from the bottom up, tucking the ends into the structure to hold them in place. Macy fed him branches as he worked. The girls piled the firewood they gathered inside the shelter. By the time Brady and Macy covered the structure, they had a significant amount of wood safe from further snow.

"How do we build a fire in the snow? And it's wet, too," Hannah said.

Brady ushered them all inside, then kneeled next to the woodpile.

"You have my knife, Mace?"

"Oh, yes." She reached in her pocket and took out the folding blade, passing it to him.

He flipped it open and picked up a piece of wood. "If we shave off the top layer, there's dry wood underneath." He scraped his knife over the wood and showed them the dry inside. "I'll shave this stuff down, but while I do that, Hannah, I need you and Macy to find a spot a few feet outside the door and dig down to the ground. Make a circle about two or three feet wide and line it with stones. We'll put the fire on top of that."

"What should I do?" Jessie asked.

"You can help me."

Macy shared a look with Brady, glad he'd given the girl a

way to rest without telling her to rest. She was just stubborn enough she would traipse around after her sister anyway.

"Come on, Hannah." She motioned the older girl outside. "Do you want to dig the pit or look for stones?"

"I'll look for stones."

"Sounds good." The girl wandered away. Macy glanced around, looking for a rock to help her dig. The snow made it difficult to tell what was what, but she found a flat rock large enough to get her hands around about ten feet from the lean-to.

With her foot, she brushed aside the snow and detritus, then crouched down and used the rock to scrape off the top layer of soil and pine needles. Hannah piled rocks next to her, which Macy laid on the bare earth to form a platform.

She stood, surveying their work. Satisfied with the result, she peered through the door at Brady. "It's ready."

He unfolded his tall frame and walked out with an armload of wood and kindling. He stopped close and leaned down. "Go check on Jessie. Her energy is really flagging."

Macy laid a hand on his arm, nodding, and walked into the shelter, crouching in front of her sister.

Jessie looked up, her brown eyes droopy.

"Are you all right?"

The girl's lip wobbled, but she nodded. "I'm okay. I'll be fine."

Macy's heart flip-flopped at the bravery Jessie showed. "Oh, sweetie. It's okay to tell me if you're hurting."

The wobble grew stronger. "It does hurt. But not so much if I don't move it. And I'm really tired."

"How about we get you some more pain medicine, then we'll make you a little bed in here and you can get some rest? Sound good?"

Jessie nodded. A single tear tracked down her cheek, and she sniffed.

A lump grew in Macy's throat. She swallowed to rid herself of it and opened Brady's pack to get the first aid kit. She found the children's pain medicine they packed and gave Jessie the appropriate dose.

"Okay, you hang out there while I clear the ground in here, all right?" There was still snow inside their shelter.

Jessie nodded again.

Macy got on her knees and started clearing snow from the far corner, pushing everything out the door. Brady walked in, carrying more pine boughs.

"Bedding," he said when she quirked a brow at him. "It might be a little pokey, but it'll be warmer than the ground."

She took the branches from him and began arranging them in the area she cleared. Once she had an area large enough for Jessie, she put her backpack on the bedding to use as a pillow and helped the girl lie down. Brady pulled out a space blanket and laid it over her.

Macy tucked it around her thin shoulders. "You get some rest."

The girl nodded, her eyes already closing.

She gave Jessie's leg a pat, then returned to helping Brady lay the floor of their shelter. They ducked outside to check on the fire once they finished.

Hannah sat cross-legged on a patch of dirt near the flames. She glanced up when they stopped beside her. "Is Jessie going to be okay?"

Macy certainly hoped so.

"She's had a rough couple days," Brady said. "I'm hopeful once she gets some rest she'll feel better."

Hannah's frown intensified. "And if she doesn't?"

"Then we'll figure that out when it happens. Right now, I think we all need to get some sleep." He held out a hand to the girl. She took it, and he pulled her up. "Go on in and lie down with your sister. Your body heat will help keep each other warm."

Macy watched her go, knowing she was worried about her little sister. So was Macy. They'd put some miles in today, but the girl had spent a lot of the trek on Brady's shoulders. She hoped it was just all catching up to her and not something more serious.

Brady's breath puffed white in front of his face as he stared into the darkness of the lean-to. He could hear Hannah and Jessie snoring softly and was glad they were getting some much needed rest. The shelter turned out better than he hoped. It provided a good break from the wind and held the heat from their bodies and from the fire outside, raising the temperature inside just enough it wasn't freezing.

Macy shifted against him, reminding him why he was still awake. After heating a few rocks near the fire, then bringing them inside to help keep them warm, they laid down with the kids, using the second space blanket for themselves. Unfortunately, that meant they had to stick close together to huddle under it. Her backside had been pressed against his front for over an hour now. He would turn away, but he knew their positions were keeping each other warm.

At first, it hadn't bothered him. They'd been focused on getting warm. But now? Now he wished he'd packed a blanket for each of them.

She sighed and rolled over to face him. "What?"

He frowned. "Huh?"

"I can hear you thinking. What?"

"Nothing."

"Bullshit. Why aren't you asleep?"

"Why aren't you?"

"Because you aren't. I can't relax when you're all tense behind me. What's bothering you?"

That was not a subject he was willing to get into. He shrugged. "Just can't sleep."

She shifted, and her thigh brushed the reason he was still wide awake. Curses flew through his mind. He'd done his best to keep that part of his anatomy from touching her, knowing it would just make things worse for him.

Macy froze. She lifted her head ever so slowly to look at him.

He swallowed, praying she would ignore it—him. It was not her fault his body reacted to her the way it did. Their situation was hardly the place for him to be imagining her naked and writhing beneath him, but his body didn't care. He could be close to dead and still want this woman.

She edged closer. Brady's muscles tensed.

"When we get back, I'll fix that." Her whispered words went straight to his groin. He pulsed behind the fly of his pants.

With a groan, he flipped her over, removing the temptation to kiss her senseless. She giggled and scooted back, her butt making contact with his hips. He groaned again, pushing her forward to make some space.

"Macy, please." His strangled plea was all he could force past his lips. It took all his concentration to keep a rein on his desire. He wanted to bury his face in her neck and run his hands all over her delectable body.

"Fine." She glanced back. "I'll behave. But all bets are off once we're home. I'm tired of the song and dance, Brady. Last week can't just be an anomaly. Something has to give." She turned around and settled into their mattress of pine needles.

Brady bit back another groan, this one of frustration, and

laid his head down. How the hell was he supposed to sleep after that? Damn woman had him tied up in knots. He just wanted to live his life. Uncomplicated. Was that so much to ask?

He shifted, trying to create more room in his pants. It was no use, though. He was destined to sleep with a hard-on tonight. With a sigh, he closed his eyes, willing his mind to shut off. If he was going to be worth anything tomorrow, he needed to rest. He forced his thoughts to more mundane things, like all the ranch stuff he needed to do once they returned. It helped, and he grew sleepy, his eyes staying closed on their own. Macy's scent drifted around him. Her earthiness and the hint of shampoo left were enough to ease him into a fitful slumber.

Several hours later, he woke with a start, glancing around the dim interior of the lean-to, unsure what roused him. It was dark. Their fire was nothing but embers now, and clouds obscured the moon and stars. The snow had stopped, but not before several inches coated the ground.

Jessie moaned and shifted, coughing in her sleep. Brady frowned, sitting up. That was new. He crawled out from under the space blanket, trying not to wake anyone else, but the crinkly material made it impossible not to make noise. Macy drew in a deep breath and sat up next to him.

"What's going on?"

"I want to check on Jessie," he whispered. "She's coughing."

"What?" She turned to look at her sister in the dim light. The little girl coughed again, sending Macy into motion. She pushed away the blanket and crawled over to her, putting a hand on her forehead.

"She's burning up, Brady."

"Dammit. I was afraid this would happen. She inhaled the river water. God only knows what was floating around in it."

"You think she has pneumonia?"

He nodded. "I wouldn't doubt it. I know it's still dark, and we only had a few hours of sleep, but we need to move. She needs a doctor."

Macy didn't hesitate. She shook Hannah awake. "Han. Wake up. We need to leave."

The girl yawned and sat up. "What? Why?"

"Jessie's feverish. We need to get back to civilization."

Hannah looked at her sister, seeing her flushed cheeks even in the darkened interior, and scrambled out of the blanket.

Jessie stirred. "Mommy?"

Macy stroked her hair. "Shh. It's Macy, sweetie. You keep resting. We're going to pack up."

"I don't feel so good."

"I know. That's why we're leaving now. You rest. We'll come get you when we're ready."

"Okay." Her eyes closed again.

Brady tugged on Macy's arm, then gestured for her to follow him outside. Once they were near the firepit, he bent his head close to hers. "She can't walk out of here, and I think she's too weak to sit on my shoulders."

"Are you going to carry her the whole way?"

"I'd like to rig up some kind of harness. Strap her to my back or something, so I have my hands free."

"We used the last of the rope for the lean-to."

"So we tear it down. I can't carry her fifteen miles over this terrain. Not if she can't hold on."

"Okay. Let's get to work, then." She ducked back into their shelter, picking up his backpack and handing it to him.

He set it down just outside, then followed her in. "Hannah, grab some of the bedding and bring it outside." He scooped Jessie into his arms.

The older girl did as he asked, and he laid Jessie on the pine boughs near the remnants of the fire, then went to help

Macy untie the rope and unwind it from the trees they fitted together. Once he had the rope free, he took it, his backpack, and one of the space blankets, and walked over to the girl.

"What's your plan?" Macy asked.

"We're going to make a bit of a papoose." He removed his pack from its aluminum frame and set it aside, then laid the frame flat, settling the space blanket over it. He took off his coat and put it over the blanket, then lifted Jessie from her makeshift bed and put her on top, still curled up, wrapping the coat and blanket around her before using the rope to secure her to the frame.

"That's kind of genius," Hannah said.

"I just hope it's not too uncomfortable for her." He gathered the extra rope, spooling it and tying it to the frame, then tipped the frame up, checking to see how much she shifted when vertical. She sagged a bit, but it was minimal. "Okay. Let's get this show on the road. Hannah, you need to wear Macy's backpack. She has to wear mine."

The girl picked up Macy's bag and slung it over her shoulders.

"Macy, help me get her on my back." He lifted Jessie, sliding one arm through the strap. Macy steadied the frame while he slid his other arm through. "Is she sitting okay?" He glanced over his shoulder, but couldn't see much.

"I think so." Macy bent to check the girl's position. "She's nestled into the bottom fairly well and her face is free of your coat and the blanket. I think you're good."

"Awesome." He clicked the waist strap into place. "You ready?"

She dumped a bunch of snow onto their fire, stirring it and adding more snow before she hefted his backpack onto her shoulders, using the other space blanket woven through the shoulder straps as a waist strap to take some of the bag's weight. "I am now. Let's go."

Brady didn't hesitate. He took off into the darkness, flashlight in his hand. He prayed the batteries held out until daybreak. Tripping over a log in the dark right now was not in his plans.

TWELVE

"Goddammit." Macy stared over the edge of the hundred-foot cliff. She was never camping in such mountainous terrain again. Her shoulders sagged, her body tired. That cliff was the final hurdle in their journey before they reached the valley floor and the town just a couple miles away.

"How do we get down? We don't have any more rope," Hannah said.

"We do, we just have to take apart Jessie's sling." Brady shrugged one arm out of his backpack frame. Macy helped him steady Jessie as he removed his other arm and lowered her to the ground.

He untied the girl from the frame, propping her against a boulder. She looked at him with glassy, feverish eyes, her cheeks still flushed despite the chill in the air.

"Are we almost home?"

"A few more miles, sweetie. You're doing great. We just need to get down this cliff and we're home free."

"Good." She coughed hard. "Cause it's hard to breathe."

Fear churned in Macy's gut. She tamped it down, knowing

it wouldn't help them. Instead, she gathered the rope and tied it around the boulder using a hitch knot through a carabiner, thankful for the rope's length, which would allow them to double it up and retrieve it at the bottom of the cliff. She tossed the rope over the side and tugged, making sure it was secure.

"We good?" Brady asked.

Macy nodded.

"Okay. You go down first. I'll lower the girls to you, then bring up the rear."

Determination overrode the fear burning a hole in Macy's belly. The knot she tied was strong. So long as she held on and Brady's hands didn't slip, she would be fine. So would Hannah.

He found his gloves in his pack, then hauled up the correct side of the rope and fashioned a sling out of it. Macy stepped forward and into the harness. It bit into her thighs and butt, but it would hold.

Brady caught her gaze for a moment as she stopped at the edge and looked up at him. Both of them realized what they were attempting was dangerous. But it couldn't be helped. They had to get to the valley below. Walking until they found another way down wasn't an option. Jessie's fever continued to climb and she wheezed now.

He cupped her cheek. "Be careful."

"I will. Don't drop me."

"Not a chance."

Macy swallowed hard at the emotion shining in his eyes. She stood on her toes and pressed a quick kiss to his lips. "I'll see you at the bottom."

He nodded, taking a deep breath, and wrapped his arms in the rope. "Ready?"

"Yep." She gripped the rope and stepped over the edge. It pinched her skin, making her wince, but she kept going.

Bruises would fade. She walked down the cliff at a steady pace, grateful for Brady's strength. In minutes, she reached the bottom and stepped out of the harness. It sailed back up the cliff as he reeled it in. A minute later, Hannah appeared over the edge. Macy watched with her heart in her throat as the girl made her way down, only breathing a sigh of relief when she could reach up and grab her.

"Let's get you out of this and get Jess down here." She helped Hannah out of the rope, then looked up. Brady stood at the edge, watching. He pulled the rope up as soon as Hannah was free.

"Are you doing okay?"

Hannah nodded. "I'm just worried about Jessie."

"Me too. But we'll get her to help soon."

"I know. It just can't happen fast enough."

That was the truth. There were ants crawling through Macy's body. She wanted Jessie down here and in the hands of medical professionals now. It would be at least an hour, though, before they reached town. But the end was in sight.

"Heads up!"

Brady's shout drew their attention. They looked up to see Jessie coming over the edge in a modified harness. He'd put a sling under her arms so she couldn't tip backward and fall out. Macy waited, shifting from foot to foot as he lowered her until she was within reach. She and Hannah grabbed the girl and guided her to the ground, removing her from the harness so Brady could pull it back up and lower himself down.

They moved away from the base to give him room. Macy stared at the top, willing him to come over soon. Jessie's breathing was worse and her color was terrible. Her lips were blue.

The rope fell over the side, dropping to the ground where they'd been standing. Brady's tall form appeared at the top, pausing only a moment before he walked over the edge. He twined the rope around his lower legs, locking his ankles over it to create a brake. He slid down at a slow, but steady pace, his arms bulging as he lowered himself hand over hand.

Part way down, his foot slipped and the rope unraveled from his legs. Macy let out a shout and stepped closer, her first instinct to catch him. His hands gripped the rope above him, sliding until he managed to halt his descent, but not before he slammed into the cliff, smacking his head on the rock.

"Brady!"

"I'm okay!" He looked down at her.

Macy could see blood on the side of his face. He wasn't okay, but she couldn't help him until he got to the bottom. "Can you not do that again?"

"Wasn't trying to the first time."

"Just get your ass down here."

He grumbled something she couldn't make out and started to descend again. Macy rummaged in his pack for the first aid kit and met him with it when his feet touched the ground. She grabbed his head before he could let go of the rope and pressed some gauze to the wound oozing blood.

"Ow. Dammit, Macy."

"Hey, I'm not the one who whacked my head on a cliff. Hold still so I can stop the bleeding." She pressed harder and he cursed again.

"I'm fine." He put his hand over hers, taking the gauze. "Just slap some butterflies on it. We need to get moving."

Macy frowned up at him, but rooted through the kit for the bandages, quickly finding them. "You need to sit or kneel. I can't reach it well enough."

He dropped to his knees. She parted his hair, finding the gash. Swabbing at it with the gauze, she cleared away more blood, then swiped an alcohol swab over it to clean it. He hissed, but didn't move. She did her best to put some butterfly closures over it, hoping they stopped the bleeding.

"I don't know how well that will hold. Your hair is in the way."

"It'll be fine." He stood. "Come on. Let's get Jessie back in the carrier and get moving. We're only a couple miles from town now."

Hannah came up and took the first aid supplies from Macy, putting them away while Brady yanked the release rope. He and Macy wrapped Jessie up and got her on Brady's back once more. They took off through the trees at a quicker pace than before. With about a mile to go, Jessie began coughing. Harsh, wracking coughs that folded her little body in on itself.

Brady stopped so Macy could check on her. To her horror, flecks of blood dotted Jessie's sleeve.

"Brady. She's coughing up blood."

"What? Fuck. Okay, let's move."

"Wait." She grabbed his arm to stop him.

"Wait? For what? We don't have time for this."

"No, we don't. Hannah and I are slowing you down. You can move faster than either of us. Run ahead. We'll meet you in town. I know the way."

"No, I don't want to leave the two of you out here by yourselves."

"We're only about a mile from town. We'll be fine. You're wasting more time by arguing."

His mouth flattened, but Macy knew she was right. He could get Jessie to help sooner on his own than by hanging back to match their pace. She knew he knew it too, from the look in his eyes.

"Dammit. I hate it when you're right. Okay. I'll let the cops know where you are and to keep an eye out for you." He touched her cheek. "Be careful, please."

Macy put her hand over his, nodding. "We will. Go."

He gave them one last long look, then took off, his long

legs eating up the ground and carrying him into the dense foliage out of view.

She looked at Hannah, who had tears coursing down her face. "Hey. Hey, she's going to be okay."

"Are you sure?"

She wasn't, but there was no way she would tell Hannah that. "Brady will get her to help in no time. The doctors will take good care of her. Come on. Let's find our way home, too."

Hannah nodded and followed her deeper into the trees.

Brady ran as fast as he dared. Jessie bounced around on his back, but didn't protest. That worried him. If she felt well, she'd be giving him hell right now for the bumpy ride. Her silence pushed him faster. His head throbbed and blood still oozed down his face, but he ignored it. His priority was reaching help.

Within fifteen minutes, he reached the edge of town, breaking through the trees into someone's backyard. He ran up to the back door and pounded on the wood, praying someone was home. He waited half a minute, but no one answered. Running around front, he surveyed the street, heading for a house with a car parked in the driveway.

He took the stairs to the porch in one stride and pressed the doorbell. Through the glass, he could see a man come around the corner. Brady breathed a sigh of relief as the door swung open.

"Can I help you?" The man stood with the door cracked and looked Brady's tall, bedraggled body up and down.

"Yes. My name's Brady Archer. My friends and I got caught in the rainstorm the other night and there was a landslide. I need you to call an ambulance." He pointed to his back. "She got caught in the river and has developed pneumonia."

The man stared at him a moment, then opened the door wider to peer around Brady's back to see the child nestled inside the makeshift papoose.

"Oh my goodness. Come in, please." He stepped back and waved him inside.

Brady stepped over the threshold and shrugged an arm out of his pack frame.

"Here, let me help." The man moved around to help get Jessie off Brady's back. They laid her on the floor, and Brady untied her. Her limbs unfolded when he released her from the ropes and blanket, limp. She opened her eyes to look at him for a brief second.

"Mommy?"

"We'll get a hold of your mom, sweetie. But you're going to take an ambulance ride first." Brady looked up at the stranger. "Where's your phone?"

"Oh, right." The man pulled a cell from his pocket and dialed 911, reporting the situation.

After he had an ambulance on the way, Brady motioned for the phone. The man handed it to him. He identified himself to the dispatcher, who expressed her relief that he and the others were safe. He thanked her and asked to be transferred to Seb.

Blowing out a breath, he ran a hand through his hair while he waited for the call to connect, feeling the sting as some of the strands tugged free from the butterflies on his scalp. His energy flagged and suddenly he could feel all his aches and pains as the adrenaline ebbed.

"Brady! Thank God. Is everyone okay?" Seb's deep voice came over the line, pulling him out of his head.

"Mostly. Jessie's pretty sick. She fell into the river and inhaled some water. Now she's running a fever and coughing.

I think she's developed pneumonia. I'm at a house in—" He broke off and looked at the stranger. "What town is this?"

"Benson."

He nodded and turned back to the phone. "I'm in Benson. Macy and Hannah are still on their way into town. Jessie's lips are blue and she's coughing up blood. We got down the cliffs to the west of town and I took off running. Other than a few bumps and bruises, the rest of us are fine."

"Jesus. There's an ambulance coming, right?"

"Yeah. Can you call Denise and have her meet us at the hospital? Wherever it is they send her? I'm guessing they might even fly her out of here to Denver. She's in bad shape, Seb."

"I'll get her there myself. You said Macy and Hannah aren't with you?"

"Not yet. They probably aren't far behind."

"I'll touch base with Benson PD and send a deputy that way as well. We'll get you all reunited."

Brady drew in a shaky breath, the adrenaline crash hitting. He swallowed hard. "Okay." Sirens sounded in the distance. "I need to go. The ambulance is almost here."

"All right. I'll see you soon. I'm glad you're okay."

"Me too. Say a prayer for Jessie."

"I will."

They bade each other farewell and hung up. Brady handed the man back his phone. "Thanks. What's your name?"

"Wally. Wally Treacher. You said there are more of you?"

Brady nodded. "I was camping with a friend and her two younger sisters. Our campsite flooded, and we bugged out in the middle of the night only to get swept off the road in a landslide."

"I heard about that. They found your car."

"I wondered if they would. We couldn't stay put, though. The water was rising."

"Yeah. It was downstream from the slide. It's amazing you all survived the fall."

"We got lucky, that's for sure." The sirens screamed to a halt outside. He peered down at Jessie, whose breathing continued to labor, while Mr. Treacher went to answer the door. The paramedic and EMT followed him into the living room. Brady moved back to give them space to work.

As he predicted, they called for a chopper to take the girl to the children's hospital in Denver. He leaned against the couch, watching them ready her for transport, when commotion at the front door drew his attention. Macy's auburn head appeared around the door. He shot to his feet, reaching her and Hannah in a few strides, enveloping them both in a hug.

"How's she doing?" Macy pulled back.

"No worse than when I left you, but she's still very sick."

Hannah took a couple steps closer, then turned to look up at Brady before walking forward and wrapping her arms around his waist. Her small shoulders shook as she held back sobs.

He hugged her close and rubbed her back. "She's in good hands now. I told you I'd get her to help."

She sniffed and looked up at him. "Thank you. Not just for getting her here, but for saving her." She hugged him again. "Thank you," she said, her voice nothing more than a wobbly whisper.

"You're welcome." He returned her hug, thankful he'd been there to help.

THIRTEEN

Macy pushed her damp hair away from her face and leaned back in the uncomfortable chair around the small table in the doctor's lounge, waiting for Hannah to finish in the shower. The paramedics insisted the three of them get checked, so they let Seb's deputy drive them to the hospital in Silver Gap, rather than the local ER. They all wanted to go home rather than be stuck in a facility over an hour away. The staff cleaned up their cuts and put some glue on Brady's head wound, then gave them each a set of scrubs and let them use the doctor's lounge to shower. Jessie was now in Denver, having been airlifted not long after Macy and Hannah reached Benson. It was too early for any news on the girl, which meant Macy was an emotional wreck. She was sure some of that was due to a lack of sleep.

The door to the men's shower opened, and Brady walked out. He, too, was dressed in green scrubs, but he looked infinitely better in them than she did. His broad shoulders stretched the seams on his top. The short sleeves showed off his powerful arms and part of his tattoos. The pants hugged his hips and muscular thighs. The entire look was ruined, though, as her eyes traveled down his legs to his feet, where his scrub pants ended about four inches above his ankles and skimmed the top of his hiking boots.

She giggled and covered her mouth to hold back more. "I'm sorry. Everything fits great except in the length."

"Go ahead and laugh. I know I look ridiculous. The nurse told me this was the best they had. Apparently, they special order longer pants for employees who need them and don't keep extras on hand."

Macy chuckled. "Well, at least you don't have to wear them for long."

"Yeah. Where's Hannah? I'm ready to go home."

"She should be out anytime. She wanted to eat before she showered, so I went first."

He walked over and sat down next to her, setting his bag of dirty clothes at his feet. "What did she eat? Real food sounds good."

"Maggie went and got her a cheeseburger."

"And she didn't get any for us?"

"Right?" She flipped a hand. "She was in with Hannah in the treatment room, so she had no idea we wanted the same thing. We can run by Boone's on the way to the ranch."

He nodded, staring straight ahead.

"Hey." She laid a hand on his thigh. "You okay?"

He looked at her. "Yeah. Just thinking about Jessie and how much she wanted a cheeseburger too. It kinda sucks she can't have it yet after all she went through."

Macy leaned over and rested her head on his shoulder. "You got her to help as fast as you could. I have faith she'll be all right."

"Me too."

To her surprise, he reached over and threaded his fingers through hers, where they rested on his leg. She wrapped her other arm around his bicep and savored the contact. The comfort he provided.

They stayed that way until Hannah emerged a few minutes later. Brady broke away from her and stood.

"You ready to go?" he asked the girl.

She nodded, clutching her bag of dirty clothes with both hands. "Are we going to Denver?"

"Not tonight," Macy said, rising. "There's nothing we can do for Jessie right now. The doctors are busy running tests and getting her on the right medicines to make her better. The best thing we can do for her is to get a good night's rest. We'll go up there tomorrow, okay?"

Hannah remained stoic, but nodded. "Okay. Where am I supposed to sleep? Mom's in Denver with Jess."

"You're both coming back to my house," Brady said.

Macy glanced up at him. That was news to her. She'd expected to stay at Denise's house with Hannah.

"Good." Hannah's shoulders relaxed. "I didn't really want to go home without Mom or Jessie. It'd be weird."

"No weirdness will happen tonight," Macy said, pushing aside her reservations about staying with Brady for Hannah's sake. She walked forward and looped an arm through the girl's, leading her to the door. "We're going to swing past Boone's so Brady and I can get something to eat, then we'll stop to get you and me some clothes before we head to his house. I can tell you, you will be very comfortable in his spare bedroom. The mattress is awesome."

Hannah cracked a smile. "That sounds great. Can I get a milkshake?"

"How are you still hungry?" Brady asked, holding the door for them and following them down the corridor. "Those burgers are huge. And I'm betting there were fries with it, too."

"There were." She smiled up at him. "I still want a chocolate shake."

He rolled his eyes, but smiled. "Fine. I'm going to have banana, though."

"Ooh, they brought that back? I want that too." Macy's mouth watered at the thought. She wished the diner kept that flavor all year. It was her favorite. She quickened her pace.

They left the hospital and headed for Brady's truck, which his dad and brother dropped off earlier. The sight of the shiny black pickup made her frown.

"Why are you frowning?" Brady asked as he unlocked the doors and they climbed inside.

"My insurance rates are going to skyrocket. First Maggie's car blows up and puts a bunch of dents and scuffs on mine, now it slides down a mountain in a landslide. It's a good thing I live in town, so I can walk to work. I'm not going to be able to afford to keep a car."

He chuckled. "It won't be that bad. None of it was your fault."

"No, but someone somewhere is going to look at my claim and wonder what kind of life I live."

"It is not dull around here, I'll grant you that." He twisted the key and pulled out of the parking lot.

After a quick stop at her house for a change of clothes, then Boone's, they were on the road to the ranch. Macy leaned her head on the window and let her eyes close. She was rapidly losing energy. She should have just stayed at her house, but one, she didn't want to leave Hannah alone. The girl would have Brady, but it wasn't the same when all you wanted was your mom. Macy was as close as she would get tonight.

And two, Macy didn't want to be alone. With no one to distract her and the silence of her house, she would toss and turn, worrying about Jessie. Having others around was soothing. When they got back to Brady's, she was going to inhale her food, then collapse on the bed and sleep for ten hours, knowing she was safe. She wasn't even going to change clothes before she flopped.

The truck bumped onto the ranch drive, and she sat up, realizing she'd dozed a bit. Brady drove past the Heartwood, only stopping to input the code to get through the gate to the main ranch. He turned into Denise's driveway.

"You know, I didn't even think about needing a key to get in. Han, do you have one?"

The girl shook her head.

"I do. Denise gave me and Declan both one in case of emergencies." Macy opened the car door. "Do you still have my car keys?"

"They're in my pack." He got out and opened the tailgate, hopping inside to locate his backpack. He found the keys and handed them to her.

She peered in the backseat at Hannah. "Do you want to come with me to get some stuff, or do you just want me to grab some things for you?"

"I'll come. I want my comfy pajamas." Hannah got out and followed Macy to the house. Brady climbed back into the truck to wait.

Macy unlocked the front door and let them in. She helped Hannah find a tote bag, and they loaded it up with pajamas, a change of clothes, and a new toothbrush. In minutes, they were back in the truck and headed down the lane to Brady's house. He pulled in the driveway and parked the truck in the garage.

The overhead door rolled down as Macy opened the car door and stumbled out. She leaned back into the truck to get her tote, milkshake, and the bag of food. Brady grabbed their backpacks from the truck bed and unlocked the inner door.

"I'm going to head to bed," Hannah said, walking into the kitchen and tossing her empty shake cup in the trash.

"Okay. I'll be in later. Unless you don't want a roommate?" Macy asked. "I can sleep on the couch."

"No, that's okay. I think I'd rather not sleep alone tonight."

Macy smiled at the girl, who was trying so hard to stay strong. She could see that all Hannah wanted to do was have a good cry. She hoped she let herself once she was alone in bed. "I'll see you in a little while, then. Goodnight."

"Night." Hannah gave her a soft smile and a wave.

"I'll show you to the guest room." Brady motioned her out of the kitchen and followed her.

Sighing, Macy found a paper plate and the ketchup from the fridge and laid out her food. She was halfway through her burger when Brady reappeared.

"I left the ketchup out for you." She pointed to the bottle on the counter from her seat at the table.

"Thanks." He put his food on a plate, adding a healthy squirt of ketchup for his fries, then joined her after putting the bottle away.

"She get settled okay?"

He nodded. "Yeah. I think she'll be asleep soon."

"That's my plan too." She stuffed some fries in her mouth and washed them down with a mouthful of banana milkshake.

"Same. I can't remember ever being so tired."

"Me, either."

Footsteps made them both turn. Hannah padded over in her stocking feet.

"I found this in Macy's backpack when I was looking for my hairbrush." She held out the digital camera.

"I forgot all about that." Brady took it from her. "I'll get it to Seb in the morning. Thanks."

The girl nodded. "Night."

"Goodnight."

Macy stared at the camera in Brady's hand. "I forgot about it too. I still don't have any idea who that could be back there."

"Neither do I. It's just one more mystery in a year full of them."

That was the truth. Silver Gap was supposed to be a quiet, uneventful place. If she wanted wild, she would have stayed in Los Angeles all those years ago when she tried her hand at acting. She sure hoped things settled down. The stress was getting to her. Getting to all of them, really.

He set the camera down and stood, walking over to the fridge to open the cabinet above it.

She frowned, wondering what he was doing before she saw the whiskey bottle in his hand.

He turned around and held it out. "Want some?"

"Hell, yes." That was the good stuff. It would ensure she dropped right off to sleep. She stood up, immediately feeling the weight of her meal. "Ugh. I'm stuffed." She laid a hand over her full belly, then took her empty plate to the trash to dispose of it.

Brady took two snifters from a cupboard and poured an inch of whiskey into each glass, then handed her one.

"To being home safe. And to the hope that Jessie makes a full recovery." He held up his glass.

"Hear, hear." She tapped hers to it, then knocked back the smooth liquor. It blazed a path to her stomach, leaving her with a fuzzy warmth.

"You're supposed to sip it, Mace."

"Too tired to sip." She set her glass in the sink.

"Good point." Brady swallowed the rest of his and put both glasses in the dishwasher. "You ready to go to bed?"

Even exhausted, she couldn't let that slide. She sent him a coy smile. "Why Brady Archer, are you propositioning me?"

Heat licked his eyes, but he dampened it as he held her gaze. "Is your mind ever out of the gutter?"

"When it comes to you? Never."

His lips flattened, and he pushed away from the counter. "Well, quit. Nothing's going to happen. Not again."

Her hand shot out to land on his chest and keep him from walking away, anger surging at his continued refusal to even consider a relationship. "Remember what I said last night? I meant it. I'm tired of the song and dance." She couldn't take it anymore. It was exhausting, and she needed more to life than flirting and the occasional inability to keep their hands to themselves. "I see this ending one of two ways."

"Which are?"

"First, we break off all contact, only interacting when we can't avoid each other, like at family gatherings. History says we end up kissing and doing—other things—otherwise, which just perpetuates this limbo area we're in. I don't know about you, but I don't like that option. Regardless of the sexual tension between us, I like you, and we've been friends a long time. I'd rather not lose that."

He frowned, staring down at her, that stoic mask in place, frustrating her as usual with his ability to give away nothing.

"And the second option?"

"You stop with this misguided notion that relationships are for other people and give us a shot. I'm not Peyton, Brady."

His frown intensified. "I know you're not. But you can't be serious. You want to throw away a lifetime of friendship because I don't want to date you?"

"No. I'm willing to walk away because if I don't, I'll never have the life I want. Pining for you doesn't get me companionship or love. Or children. It gets me stress and loneliness. I can't do it anymore." And she couldn't. Watching her friends live her dream of marriage and family was slowly killing her inside. Holding Tara's twins, seeing the love and joy on her friend's face as she looked at her newborn babies, made Macy realize she wanted that. She wasn't content to be the cool aunt. She knew she could love Brady given half a chance, but if he couldn't love her back, she needed to move on.

"And you think you can find that with someone else around here? Like who?"

Macy shrugged. "There are a few other eligible men besides you in the area. And some who live elsewhere. Asa Mitchell asks me out every time he comes to town."

Brady's nostrils flared. "You can't seriously tell me you'd be willing to move back to L.A. for him. You hated it there."

"Part of the reason I hated it was because I was trying to be someone I wasn't. I was always looking to land a role, and that meant I had to act a certain way. I couldn't be me and still get jobs. All the producers saw was this sultry redhead with perky boobs. I quickly learned they didn't want me for the serious roles, and if I dared show off my intelligence, I didn't even get the airhead ones. If I move back there, it will be on my terms. I can live anywhere if I'm with the man I love."

He scoffed. "And you think Asa could be that man?"

"I don't know if he could. But I sure as hell will never find out if I keep holding out for you."

Brady pursed his lips, his eyes hard. "Well, I don't know what to tell you. I don't want to give up on our friendship. I like what we have. But I can't be the man you want. If chasing Asa is what will make you happy, go for it."

It wouldn't. She had a sneaking suspicion no one but Brady would ever make her truly happy. But she had to do something, because she couldn't continue living like this. Tears formed in her eyes. "I'm sorry. I just can't be the friend you want and be happy. It hurts too much." She sniffed, emotionally and physically drained. She was done with everything and just wanted to sleep now. "I'm going to bed. London said Seb took Denise to the hospital when I talked to her earlier, so I'll take her car to drive Hannah to Denver in the morning." She tried to smile, but it wobbled. "Thanks for keeping us alive."

"Macy—"

She held up a hand, holding onto her emotions by a thread. Exhaustion had her normal iron willpower down to nothing. If she didn't cut him off now, he could very well talk her into something she was dead-set against. "Goodnight."

His whispered reply followed her out the door.

FOURTEEN

The cold, gray sky mirrored Brady's mood as he yanked open the door to the police station. He'd awakened before the sun to get back into his routine of ranch chores after tossing and turning most of the night, thinking about Macy's ultimatum. When he came home for breakfast, she and Hannah were gone.

Now he was just pissed. He never asked her to be attracted to him. To hope for more than friendship. She wanted to ruin their friendship because she couldn't get over him? He supposed he should be flattered, but that's not how he felt. He was just... angry. At her for ruining everything. And at himself for letting things get out of hand that night and not making it clear sooner that he couldn't be the man she needed.

"Hi, Brady." Alaina Wilder smiled at him from behind the plexiglass, then frowned as she took in the thunderclouds on his face. "Everything okay?"

"Yeah. Sorry. I didn't sleep well."

Her face softened. "I heard about Jessie. How's she doing?"

"Improving." For which he was thankful. He might have

missed Macy and Hannah before they left, but that didn't mean he wasn't keeping tabs on the girl's condition. He called Declan for an update while he ate. Jessie was in the ICU, but she was stable.

"That's good. You here to see Seb?"

He nodded.

She slid the sign-in sheet toward him. He wrote his name on it, then took the visitor's badge she handed him. "Thanks."

"Yep. Let me know if there's anything I can do for Denise and the girls."

"I will."

She smiled and buzzed him through.

His long legs ate up the floor as he walked down the hallway to Seb's office. He pushed open the door, which was cracked. Seb looked up, surprise on his face as he recognized his visitor.

"Hey. What's up? Is Jessie okay?" He started to rise.

Brady waved him back down and sat across from him. "She's fine. Holding her own. That's not why I'm here."

"Okay." Seb frowned. "Why are you here, then?"

He took the kids' camera from his coat pocket. "In all the chaos yesterday, we forgot about what we found in the cave we took shelter in."

Seb took the camera, looking at it. "You found a camera?"

"No. That's Hannah and Jessie's. The cave we stayed in was deep, but it narrowed after fifty feet or so before it opened back up. Macy and I couldn't fit past that point, but the girls could. They went exploring and found a skeleton."

"Oh, you've got to be kidding. *More* bodies?"

Brady nodded. "I know. I don't know what to make of it. Hannah took pictures of the skeleton and the area where it sat. The body's small. Maybe a tiny woman or a young teenager. The clothing looks male."

Seb sighed and turned on the camera to take a look at the

pictures. He clicked through them, the frown on his face deepening with each image. "You're right. It looks like a young teenage boy." He turned it off and laid it on his desk, pressing the heels of his hands to his eyes before running his fingers through his hair. "Okay. I'll call Katie and Alex and get them out there. You or Macy are going to have to lead us there, though. Unless you wrote down the exact coordinates?"

Brady grimaced. "No. But I've got a pretty good idea where it is."

"Good. I'll get a team mobilized, but it'll probably be tomorrow before we can go. Can you get away for the day?"

"Yeah. I wasn't supposed to come back for a couple days yet, so we're good. Dad wouldn't care anyway for something like this."

"No. He'd shove you out the door."

Brady smiled, knowing Seb was right. "I just have one request, though. Can we take ATVs? I'm done hiking for a while."

Seb chuckled. "Sure."

"We'll need climbing equipment, too. The entrance isn't ground level."

"You free-climbed to get into a cave?" Seb's eyebrows shot up.

Brady shrugged. "Didn't really have a choice. We were freezing and needed to dry out from our dip in the river."

"I still can't believe you all survived that. I'm thankful, but still shocked."

"You and me both. When the mountainside gave way and we started to slide, I thought that was it. The tree we hit on the way down saved our lives. And sheer determination got me out of the river with Jessie. I wasn't about to let her die." Memories of seeing the girl's terrified face pop above the raging floodwaters flashed in his mind. He pushed them away. That was over, and it wouldn't do to dwell on it.

"No, you would sacrifice your own life before letting that happen."

He would. Not just because she was young and depended on him to keep her safe, but because it would devastate Macy if he didn't. He couldn't let her down.

His frown returned. Dammit. Why couldn't he keep her out of his thoughts?

"Got something else on your mind?"

"What?" His eyes snapped to Seb's.

"You're frowning. Pretty fiercely. Why?"

Brady shifted in his seat, not ready to talk about Macy's ultimatum. "No reason. Just memories."

Seb stared at him, his expression telling Brady he didn't believe him. "If you say so."

Agitation made Brady's leg bounce. Hell. "Why do women have to be so complicated?" The words popped out before he could stop them.

"Macy?"

"Yes. She gave me what amounts to an ultimatum. We date —seriously—or we're done. No more friendship; we act like the other doesn't exist."

"Whoa."

"Yeah. Says she can't live the life she wants if she's pining after me. That she wants love, a family." He scoffed. "She thinks she can find that with Asa Mitchell. Can you believe that? She'd be miserable back out in L.A."

"She's going out with Asa?"

"Maybe. She said he keeps asking, but she always says no. If she and I don't date, she's going to say yes. And probably not just to him. I got the feeling she's going to jump head first into the dating pool."

"There are several single men in the county near her age."

Brady waved a hand. "I'm not worried about them. I

know most of them, and they're all dirtbags with criminal records and several ex-wives."

"Knox isn't."

A jolt of jealousy and betrayal stabbed Brady in the heart, even though Knox had never shown any sort of attraction to Macy. "He wouldn't."

Seb shrugged and leaned back in his chair. "I don't know, Brady. Macy's a beautiful woman. Maybe he's just waiting to know you're out of the picture before he makes his move."

Brady's knee bounced harder, and his eyebrows dipped low in a fierce frown.

"I think you need to think about why that thought bothers you so much. If you really have no designs on her, it shouldn't matter to you who she ends up with. As a friend, you should want her to be happy. And Knox and Asa are both good guys."

"Asa's a playboy."

Seb shrugged. "Maybe a little, but he's a good man. He'd be faithful to her, I'm sure."

Brady growled and rubbed a hand over his beard. "You're right. I shouldn't care."

"But you do."

"Fuck. Yes, I do." He looked out the window, not seeing the scenery, but a pair of indigo eyes instead.

"So, what are you going to do about it?"

"I don't know. I don't want to lose her, but relationships aren't my thing."

"That's bullshit. You're already in a relationship."

"Huh? What do you mean?"

"When was the last time you were with a woman?"

Brady's cheeks reddened as the image of Macy against the wall entered his mind. And before that, he realized he hadn't wanted to hook up with anyone for nearly a year. Ever since things started to go haywire around the county.

Seb's eyes widened. "Holy shit. Did you?"

Brady stared at him, not answering.

"Well, hell. Why deny that you're together, then?"

"Because we're not. It was one time."

"Uh-huh. And before and after that, when you got the urge for that sort of thing, who pops into your head? Some faceless woman?"

He didn't like where this conversation was going. "No."

"It's Macy, isn't it?"

He shifted in his seat. "Maybe."

"Right, so, add that to your friendship and the fact you already had sex and tell me it doesn't equate to a relationship."

Brady clenched his jaw, staring at his brother with hard eyes. "It's not like that."

Seb rolled his eyes. "Get your head out of your ass and admit to yourself you want to be with her. Your life, and hers, will be much happier and less stressful if you do."

The thought of being in a committed relationship dredged up thoughts of Peyton and the devastation he felt when she admitted she cheated on him from the start and only married him for the lifestyle his money could provide. It made his skin crawl.

"I can tell what you're thinking. Don't compare Macy to Peyton. They're such polar opposites there is no comparison."

"They're not that different. Both lively and outgoing. Neither of them mind being the center of attention."

"True, but Macy rarely seeks it out. It's just her nature to take command of a room. Peyton had to be the center of attention. And, no offense, but Peyton was a bitch. Everyone could see it except you."

Which is precisely why he was so leery of getting involved with another woman. What if he was wrong again?

"Can I give you a piece of advice?"

"Sure."

"Ask yourself if you really want to be Mom and Dad's age or older and alone. No wife, no kids, no grandkids. Is that what you really want? Don't let your fear of the what ifs jeopardize your future."

Brady stared at Seb. He'd never put it in that context before. Anytime he thought of a relationship, it was always how it would affect his life in the present. Thinking about how he would feel thirty years from now never crossed his mind. It definitely merited some thought.

Seb waved a hand. "I can see I got the wheels turning, so my job is done. Get out of here, so I can get an expedition team together to collect the body you found."

He stood. "Thanks for making my life *more* complicated."

Seb grinned. "That's what brothers are for."

He rolled his eyes. "You sound like Thomas. I'll see you later. Let me know about tomorrow."

"Will do." He picked up the phone as Brady turned and walked out the door.

Brady ran a hand through his hair as he walked back to the front of the building, his thoughts in a washing machine. He still didn't know what to do about Macy's ultimatum, but for the first time in over a decade, he was seriously considering giving up his bachelor status.

The alarm on Jessie's IV pump blared, making Macy jump.

"That thing did that all night," Denise said. Dark circles under her eyes and the deepened lines on her face attesting to the truth of her statement. "It gets air in it and sets off the sensor. Sometimes, she rolls and kinks the line. It's never ending."

A nurse walked in and punched a button to silence the alarm, then smiled at them and left.

"They don't do anything about it?"

"Only if it's kinked. If it's air, they usually just silence the alarm. Sometimes they flick it to break up the bubbles. It has to be a lot of air to cause any problems. I asked. The machines are really sensitive."

The door opened again, admitting Daniel Kerr. He held a drink carrier with several cups of coffee and a soda. Macy had been surprised to see him when she arrived with Hannah this morning, but Denise said he showed up late last night and hadn't left.

"It's not Peppy Brewster, but it'll keep you awake." He walked over to Denise and handed her a cup of coffee, then sat down beside her on the couch.

Macy thanked him for the cup he held out to her. He smiled, then passed the soda to Hannah. She took a sip, noting the slightly burned taste. No, it definitely was not her coffee.

"Anything new?" he asked.

"No. She's still the same. The doctor should be in anytime, though," Denise said.

Macy's phone rang, and she dug it out of her sweatshirt pocket. Seb's name scrolled over the screen. She answered it.

"Hey. What's up?"

"Is Hannah with you?"

"Yeah, why?"

"Put her on. I need to ask her about some of these pictures she took."

"Oh, okay. I'll put you on speaker. Hang on." She pulled the phone away from her ear and looked at Hannah. "Seb needs to ask you some questions about the skeleton in the cave."

Hannah nodded.

"Skeleton?" Denise and Dan both asked.

Macy held up a finger as she put Seb on speakerphone. "Okay, Seb, go ahead."

"So, I've looked over the images you took, and my question is, did you see anything else in there with the body, or signs of another person? The cave looks like it goes back a ways, so the images fade to black. Did you go any further? See anything else that didn't belong?"

Hannah bit her lip as she thought. "I remember seeing some trash—like candy wrappers or something. It was small. But we didn't look at it too closely. We just kinda looked to see if there were any other bodies. I don't remember seeing anything else."

"What about a backpack?"

"No. I don't remember seeing one."

"How about another entrance? Did you see daylight anywhere?"

"No. It was dark as far back as we went. We didn't stray too far, though. We didn't want to get lost."

"Okay. That helps. Thank you."

"You're welcome. How are you going to get that person out of there? I barely fit through the passage."

"Our forensic tech is pretty slender. I have a deputy who's small, too. We'll figure it out. How's your sister?"

"About the same. She woke up a bit this morning."

"That's good."

"Seb, It's Kerr. Where's this body? What do you know about it so far?"

There was a pause. Macy could just see Seb's face as he processed the fact Dan was at Jessie's bedside.

Seb cleared his throat. "Kerr, what are you doing there?"

"Supporting Denise. Now, answer my questions."

Macy arched a brow. He did not want to be deterred.

Seb blew out a breath. "Macy and Hannah can probably tell you more than I can. We don't know anything yet except what the pictures show. The remains are skeletonized and the clothing looks dated, so whoever it is has been there a long time. I showed the images to Alex Randall, and he agrees it looks like a young teenage male."

A furrow formed between Kerr's eyebrows. "A teenage male, you say?"

"Yeah." Seb drew out the word. "I know that tone. You know something?"

"Maybe." Dan shifted and looked at them. "Macy, you're probably a bit too young to remember, but almost forty years ago, a local boy disappeared. His parents went to wake him up for school one morning and he was just gone. Authorities searched high and low, but found no sign of him. The consensus was he ran away. His backpack and some clothes were gone, and his window was open."

"He would have been a little older than you," Denise said. "Did you know him?"

Dan nodded. "He was my best friend's older brother."

"I'll look into it," Seb said. "What's the kid's name?"

"Steven. Steven Knight."

"Knight? Wait. Is he related to Robbie Knight?"

"Yes. Robbie was my best friend."

Macy's eyes widened. Robbie was a known alcoholic and rabble-rouser in the county. That he had once been friends with the ultra-composed Kerr was a shock.

Dan's eyes met hers. "He wasn't always the man he is now. Steven's disappearance set him down a self-destructive path. By the time we graduated high school, we weren't friends anymore. He—and his parents—were never the same."

"Do you think he knows more than he let on?" Seb asked.

"I'm not sure. If he does, he's never said anything to me."

"Okay. I'm going to go find him and ask. Thanks for the info."

"Of course. And Sheriff? When you talk to him, I'd like to be present. He might open up to me when he won't to you or your deputies."

"I'm not sure—"

Kerr cut him off. "If it turns out the body in the cave is Steven Knight, I'm recusing myself from the case. You won't have to worry about conflict of interest."

Seb was silent for a moment. "Okay. You better get back here, though. I'm going out looking for him now."

"I'm on my way. Thank you."

"See you soon." Seb hung up.

Macy turned off her phone and stowed it in her pocket, still shell-shocked.

Dan stood. "I need to go." He laid a hand on Denise's shoulder. "Call me later or if anything changes?"

Denise nodded.

He bent and pressed a kiss to the top of her head, then gathered his coat and left.

"Well, damn." Macy stared after him. "I feel like I woke up to a real-life case of body snatchers."

Denise giggled. "He really isn't as uptight as you think."

"I'm rapidly learning that. I guess he's just very quiet, and it's translated to cold and reserved. What happened with him while we were gone?"

A pretty blush stole over Denise's cheeks. She glanced at her daughter, then at Macy. "I accepted his dinner invitation. He took me to the Heartwood, and we had a wonderful time. He's so smart—smarter than anyone I've ever met— but he's kind. And he treats me like a queen. I hardly know what to make of it. Cole only did that when he wanted something. I keep waiting for the other shoe to drop. For some horrible skeleton to pop out of the closet when I least expect it." She covered her mouth. "Oh, I'm sorry. That was in poor taste."

Macy smiled and patted her hand. "It's okay. It's just an expression, but I understand what you mean. For your sake, I hope he is exactly as he seems."

"Me too. I like him. A lot." She looked at Hannah again, who gave her mother an encouraging smile.

"I hope he is, too. I don't know him well, but he does seem nice. I just want you to be happy. Seeing you happy makes me happy."

Denise pulled the girl into her and gave her a hug. "Thank you. I want that too. For me and for you and your sister." She placed a kiss on Hannah's temple. "I guess time will tell if Dan's good for the three of us. I hope he is, but if not, he gets the boot. I won't go down that route again. I've learned my lesson from your dad."

Hannah hugged her back. She pulled away as the door opened again, admitting the doctor and her staff.

"Ms. James," the woman stepped forward and held out a hand. "I'm Dr. Jordan. We spoke briefly last night."

Denise stood and took her hand. "Yes. I remember." She looked at Hannah and Macy. "This is my other daughter, Hannah, and their older sister and my friend, Macy."

Dr. Jordan looked at Macy and frowned. "These two girls are your siblings? Ms. James is your stepmother?"

"Not exactly." Macy rose to stand next to Denise. "My father ran out on my brother and me when we were teenagers. He met Denise shortly after. She was just out of high school. They never married, but have three children together."

"I see. And where is your dad?" She motioned to Macy and both girls.

"In jail."

The doctor's eyes widened. "Oh, I'm sorry."

"Don't be. He deserves to be there. It's complicated, but suffice it to say, it's where he belongs. He will not be getting out—likely ever."

"Okay, then. So, I guess any medical decisions about Jessie's care fall directly to you?" She looked at Denise.

"Yes."

"All right. How about we discuss what's going on, then?" She gestured for them to have a seat.

They returned to the couch. Denise folded her hands in her lap, twirling her thumbs as she waited for the doctor to begin.

"So, as you know, Jessie's x-rays showed some significant pneumonia, and we tested her bronchial secretions for pathogens. Early results show a couple different types of bacteria, both of which are covered by the broad-spectrum antibiotic we started her on when she arrived. We're going to change the medication, though, to target them specifically. They'll still be intravenous for now, so that won't change. I have to say, I'm very impressed with your daughter's ability to fight her infection. We were sure we would need to intubate her, but the oxygen helped dramatically. If she continues to improve the way she has, she should be out of the ICU and in a regular room in a day or two. She's still on quite a bit of oxygen, so I'd like to monitor her here at least one more day."

"Oh, that's great news." Denise glanced at Macy, who smiled.

"You have a very tough little girl, Ms. James. I think she's going to be just fine."

Tears welled in Denise's eyes. Macy felt a few of her own gather as relief hit her hard.

"Thank you, doctor." Denise sagged, gathering Hannah close.

"You're very welcome. I'm going to look her over quick, then I'll be out of your hair." She took her stethoscope from around her neck and leaned over the sleeping child to listen to her heart and lungs.

"She sounds better. The meds are working. She's still very sick, but we're moving in the right direction. Do you have any questions for me?"

"Her wrist. What's being done about it?" Macy asked.

"The break was clean, so I imagine orthopedics will put a cast on it in the next few days. The priority was stabilizing her. We've done that, so now other treatments can progress."

They thanked the doctor, and she and her team left.

Denise blew out a breath. "That was encouraging."

"It was. I think with some time, she'll be good as new."

Tears tracked down Denise's cheeks. She sniffed and waved a hand. "Sorry. I've just been through a gamut of emotions in the last few days. And I haven't slept much. I'm fine."

Macy moved to take Dan's vacated seat and wrapped an arm around her. "Cry all you want. Bottling it up isn't healthy."

She sniffed again. "I know. But I really am fine. I'm just very thankful you're all okay."

"Me too. I never want to do that again."

"Me, either," Hannah said. "I think I'm done camping."

"Nah. We just need to make sure there isn't a raindrop in sight next time."

"Yes, please."

They chuckled, the relief that the antibiotics were working and Jessie was doing better dispelling some of the tension they all felt.

Macy gave Denise one last squeeze and stood. "I'm going to go call Declan and let him know the good news. Can I get either of you anything while I'm gone?"

"Lunch?" Hannah pointed to the clock. "It's been a long time since the bagel I had this morning before we left Brady's."

Macy looked at the clock, both to check the time and to hide her reaction at the mention of his name. She was still a little shocked at the things she said last night. Sleep deprivation, worry, and a healthy dose of sexual frustration had combined to create the perfect storm to put her emotions in a tailspin. And while she would regret the loss of his friendship, she wouldn't regret the freedom that came with moving on.

She was done pining for a man who was never going to change.

"I can do lunch. What do you want?"

"Just a sandwich is fine. And chips."

"Sounds good. Denise, do you want anything?"

"The same, please."

"Okay. I'll be back." She picked up her purse and left the room, finding a quiet alcove to call her brother with an update.

Coughing greeted her when he answered.

"Sorry." He coughed again. "You caught me mid coughing fit. What's up?" His normally deep voice was raspy.

"Maybe you should go to the doctor. You sound terrible."

"I already did. Believe it or not, I feel better than I did a couple days ago."

"You're right, I don't believe it. But I'm glad. Anyway, I called to give you an update. The doctor was just in for rounds. She said Jessie's improving, and they've identified the bacteria causing her pneumonia, so they're going to switch up her antibiotics for a more targeted treatment. She said she hopes to step down her oxygen and put her in a regular room in a day or so."

"That's great. How are the rest of you holding up?"

"We're good. Denise is a lot more relaxed now that Jessie seems to be out of the woods, even though she's still pretty sick. Oh! You'll never guess who was here when Hannah and I got here." She paused for dramatic effect. "Daniel Kerr."

"What? Why?"

"He and Denise are dating."

"Are you serious? What does she want with a prick like him?"

"He's not the prick we think he is. He's just really quiet and reserved. I'm sure he still has some asshole tendencies—I remember Seb saying how he was looking out for his election chances when you were arrested before, but he backed down. Part of it is, he just can't show favoritism or be soft when it comes to his job."

"I get that, but I still don't like the guy."

"Well, you should probably try, because I think he's going to be hanging around a while. She really likes him. And from what I saw, he really likes her, too."

Declan sighed. "Fine. Hey, why did Brady call me for an update this morning instead of you?"

Macy fought the urge to groan. Why couldn't she get away from him? She cleared her throat. "We're not on the best of terms at the moment."

Silence as loud as church bells came over the line.

"Why?"

"Because he's a dumbass, and I'm tired of waiting on him to change."

He sighed. "I get that, but we do still have to see him on a fairly regular basis."

"I know, and I'll be civil. I just won't go out of my way to spend time with him or talk to him."

"God, this is going to go so well."

"It'll be fine. I'm not worried." But worry churned in her gut anyway. She didn't want to alienate any of her friends because she didn't want anything to do with Brady. It couldn't be helped, though. The choice she made was for her mental wellbeing. She wouldn't pretend things wouldn't be rocky at first, but eventually, they'd get used to the new normal.

"I need to go. I promised Denise and Hannah I'd bring them lunch." Her own stomach grumbled. She hadn't been hungry when they woke up. Too much going on in her head. But she was now.

"Okay. But, Mace? Don't give up on Brady yet. He's just scared. Peyton's betrayal did a number on him."

She pinched the bridge of her nose, feeling some sympathy

creep back in for Brady's position. *No.* If she waffled, she would end up right back where she started. She dropped her hand. "I'm not waiting on him anymore. My life is mine, and I'm going to make the best of it. I'll talk to you later."

Declan sighed again, but didn't argue. "Yeah, okay. Bye."

"Bye." She took the phone away from her ear and smashed the end call button, frustrated. She knew cutting Brady from her life wouldn't be easy. She hoped her friends understood why she had to do it more than Declan did. Maybe one day they could be friends again, but right now, she needed a clean break.

She let out a growl, releasing some of her frustration, and stepped out of the alcove, determined to shove thoughts of the man to the depths of her brain. Food. That was what she needed to focus on. And her sister. Not deep, dark eyes, a soft beard, and muscles for days.

Heat crept up her neck as she remembered Brady in his scrubs. *Dammit.*

Fifteen

An icy wind blew down Brady's collar as he left the barn and walked to his truck. He hunched deeper into his coat and lengthened his stride. Normally, he didn't mind the cold, but he'd had enough of it until next winter.

Inside, he started the engine and cranked up the heat, warming his hands over the vents before buckling up and heading down the drive to leave the ranch. Seb asked him to stop by the station this evening to go over the game plan for tomorrow, as well as a map of the area.

He turned left onto the main road and settled into his seat for the fifteen-minute drive. Scenery whizzed past as he sped down the straight section of road before it turned curvy. The road rose sharply as he reached the hills. He wound through the curves, gaining speed as he went down the other side of the mountain. He pressed the brake to slow. A warning light blared on his dash.

"What the hell?" He glanced at the little red brake icon. What was that about? The truck leaned into the curve and he pressed harder on the brake. The pedal went to the floor, and the truck didn't slow.

"Shit." He'd lost his brakes. Thinking fast, he cut the engine and pulled the hand brake. The truck fishtailed as he steered around the bend. He maneuvered to the berm, and the vehicle rocked to a halt on the side of the road.

"Holy fuck." Hands shaking from the close call, he stepped out of the car, needing to move as adrenaline continued to course through his veins. After pacing several yards away, he turned to stare at the pickup, wondering what happened. It was only two years old.

With long strides, he walked back, crouching next to the tires to look at the brakes through the rim. Not seeing anything, he retrieved his jack from the toolbox on the back and lifted the rear axle, then wiggled underneath. He took out his phone, using its flashlight function so he could see. The pads and shoes looked fine. He shined the light on the brake lines and followed it up to the front, but nothing stood out.

Perplexed, he wiggled back out and stood up. He turned off the flashlight and called Seb.

"Hey, you almost here? We're ready to start the briefing."

"I'm stuck on the highway. My brakes went out."

"What? Are you all right?"

"I'm fine. My emergency brake worked, but I'm stranded."

"Okay. Call a wrecker, and I'll come get you. Text me when the tow truck arrives."

"Sounds good. Thanks."

"Yep." Seb hung up.

Brady looked up the number to a local towing service and called it, getting a driver dispatched to him.

He took a deep breath, blowing it out as he looked around. *Hell.* Could his day get any worse?

An hour later, his truck on its way back to the ranch and their mechanic, he climbed out of Seb's pickup and followed him into the police station. Their boots thudded on the tile floor as they walked to the conference room where Alex and Katie waited. He entered the room, a deep scowl on his face, and took a seat.

Silence greeted him. He looked to his left at Katie, who'd stopped talking to Alex when he came in.

"What?"

She held up both hands. "Nothing."

"What crawled up your ass?" Alex asked.

He huffed. "Sorry. I've had a bad day."

"Ignore him. He's being moody." Seb sat down next to him. "Let's get this meeting going, shall we? I'd like to go home and see my wife before she goes to bed."

Brady would just like to *go* to bed. Maybe tomorrow would be a better day. He had a nagging feeling it wouldn't, though.

He pushed his negative thoughts away and sat forward, rolling open the map on the table to look at it. The others crowded closer. He found the spot where he thought the cave was. "We're going here. Roughly. The campground is up here." He pointed to a spot higher in the mountains. "The landslide was here." He pointed to a different spot down the road from their camp. "We walked back up the slope, trying to find a way out, but the terrain just kept getting steeper. I think we came out of the river somewhere around here." He indicated a spot downstream. "From there, we walked into the forest, looking for the cave system Macy researched before we left, which we found in this area." He circled a spot with his finger.

"Jesus, how do we get there?" Alex asked.

"Same way we got out. We go over land from Benson. It's the closet place. But we're taking ATVs. I'm not walking."

"How far away is it?" Katie asked.

"Fifteen, twenty miles, maybe."

"That's going to be a haul with equipment. We may have to overnight," she replied.

"It's not supposed to rain again, is it?"

Seb chuckled. "We'll bring a cover for your tent, just in case."

"Appreciate it."

They went over some more details before agreeing to meet at the ranch at five tomorrow morning.

Katie stood and stretched. "It's too bad Peppy Brewster isn't open that early. I'm going to need a big jolt in the morning."

"It wouldn't matter. Macy closed the café for a few days. She wanted to make sure Jessie was okay before she came back."

Brady paused to look at his brother as he rose from the table. That was news to him.

Seb noticed his surprised look. "What, you didn't know that?"

He shook his head.

"Man, you need to set things right with her."

"Haven't exactly had time to do that today."

"Did you at least think about what I said earlier?"

"Yes."

"And?"

"And it's none of your business. Can we go home? I'm exhausted."

Seb's mouth flattened, but he kept his opinion to himself, for which Brady was grateful. He really did not want to discuss his relationship with Macy with anyone right now. He didn't even want to think about it himself. He needed some rest to be able to gain any perspective on the issue. His brain was fried.

"Yeah, let's go."

Alex and Katie walked out ahead of them, and they parted

ways in the parking lot. Brady hopped into the passenger seat of Seb's truck and buckled up, leaning his head against the seat and closing his eyes.

"You okay?"

"Yeah. I don't want to talk, Seb. Just drive, please."

It took several moments for Brady to realize Seb continued to sit there. Without starting the vehicle. He opened his eyes and looked at his brother. "What?"

"Dude, I don't know what's wrong with you, but you need to get that shit figured out. Surly Brady is not cool."

Brady's lips thinned, but he just stared at Seb in the darkened interior of the truck.

"Whatever's eating at you—whether it's Macy or something else—you need to deal with it."

"I just want to sleep." He pointed at the ignition. "Can't do that sitting here."

Seb shook his head and cranked the engine. "Fine. Be an asshole. It's no wonder Macy washed her hands of you."

Brady gritted his teeth. *He* was not the problem. *He* never asked for any of this. Why couldn't people leave things as they were? Why did stuff have to change? He scrubbed a hand over his face. He wasn't ignorant of the fact life changed. It didn't mean he had to like it, though.

"Look, I've never been one to—be able to express my emotions well. And it's harder when I don't get the chance to decompress. I'm not trying to be a jerk. I just need some time to rest and to just breathe."

Seb sighed. "Yeah, okay. Sorry. I know you need your space. I just don't want to see you let something—someone— great slip through your fingers."

"I know. And I *am* going to think about what you said."

"Good." He put the truck in gear and pulled out of the station.

"Thanks for taking me home. Hopefully, whatever's wrong with my truck is easily fixable."

"You said the brakes gave out? With no warning?"

"Yeah. I went around a curve, tapped the brake, and my warning light came on. I pressed harder and my foot went to the floor. There was just nothing."

"That's strange."

"You're telling me. I know I work that truck hard, but I don't know how the brakes failed. Unless I kicked up a sharp rock somewhere and poked a hole in the line. I didn't see anything when I looked, but all I had for light was my phone."

"Liam will figure it out, I'm sure."

Brady had faith in their mechanic too. It was just weird.

Seb's radio crackled to life.

"Sheriff, do you copy?"

He picked up the mic and pressed the button to talk. "Dispatch, this is Archer. Go ahead."

"We just got a 911 call from Macy Briggs. Someone broke into her house. She requested we call you."

Brady's heart thundered in his chest.

Seb's tires squealed on the asphalt as he hit the brakes and turned around. "Is she okay? Over."

"She's fine. I've dispatched a deputy to take a report."

"Okay. I'm on my way. Archer out." He hung up the mic and pressed the gas. "You awake now?" He glanced at Brady.

"Yes. Can't you go any faster?"

"There's no siren on this vehicle, so no."

Brady's jaw worked, and he stared out the window, willing the car to get to Macy's faster. In reality, only a couple minutes went by, but it felt five times that long before they pulled up to the curb in front of Macy's house. He was out of the car before Seb cut the engine, running through the yard to the front door.

"Macy?" He skidded to a halt just inside the door as his brain registered the message on the wall. "What the fuck?"

"Brady?"

He turned to see Macy rising from a chair at her dining table, where she huddled with Hannah. He hurried over and enveloped her in a hug, relief that she appeared to be okay making his hands shake. "Are you two all right? What's going on?"

"We came home to an open door and that on the wall." She motioned to the words spray painted on the living room wall. "What are you doing here?"

"I was with Seb when he got the call."

"Oh."

"Hey, Macy." Seb walked up, Deputy Gentry on his heels. "Any idea who would do that?"

Brady looked at the words again. *Back off or you're next.* The words, painted in red, dripped down the wall like blood. Ice filled his veins as the context slapped him in the face.

"Do you think this has something to do with the skeleton we found? I mean, I know we haven't broadcast it, but Seb's been planning a retrieval. Something like that wouldn't stay quiet around here."

"It's possible," Seb said. "And you guys are the only ones who know its location." He glanced at them. "Macy, maybe you and Hannah should come back to the ranch. I know you —want your own space." His eyes flicked from her to Brady before he continued. "But it's safer out there."

She rolled her lips in, then nodded and put an arm around Hannah. "That's fine. I just need to get some clothes. I don't really want to stay here with that written on the wall."

"Understandable." He glanced at Gentry. "Have you checked the rest of the house? Is anything else disturbed?"

Gentry shook his head. "No. It was just the busted door lock and that." He tipped his head toward the wall.

"Okay. Macy, go get what you need, but keep an eye out for anything amiss. If you see anything, don't touch it and let us know. I think there's probably a crime scene tech on the way." He arched a brow in question at Gentry, who nodded.

"Pack for a few days," Brady said as she stepped away. "It'll take me that long to get over here and repaint your wall."

She frowned at him, opening her mouth to say something, then changed her mind and walked away, shaking her head. He knew she was likely confused. Hell, so was he. She'd all but cut him out of her life last night. He hadn't explicitly said he was all in on this dating thing, but he was acting like things were all good between them. He wasn't about to walk away from her, though, when she needed him. If she wanted to kick him to the curb, she could do it after they figured out who painted that message on her wall.

Macy reappeared carrying a small backpack.

"Ready?" Seb asked.

She nodded.

He led them out the door to the cars. Brady stopped beside Denise's SUV and held out a hand for the car keys. Macy stared up at him as Hannah got in the passenger seat.

"No."

He frowned and dropped his hand. "What do you mean, no?"

"I mean, you can ride with Seb. I'll drive us back."

He opened his mouth to protest, but she held up a hand.

"Don't. I meant what I said. Unless you've changed your mind, I'm done."

Brady stayed silent. His brother's advice and his feelings for this woman bounced around his brain, never stopping long enough for him to get a handle on anything. Some of the fatigue he felt earlier crept back in.

"That's what I thought. It might be best if we just stay at Denise's tonight." She reached for the door handle.

He put a hand over the frame to keep her from opening it. "No. You're staying with me."

"You're leaving at the butt crack of dawn. What difference will it make?"

"A lot. At that point, there will be activity on the ranch. But in the intervening hours? The gate and cameras aren't foolproof. We've seen that."

Her nostrils flared as she glared up at him. "Fine. But I'm still driving myself." She plucked his hand off the door frame and let herself in the car.

He stepped back, casting one last look at her before jogging to Seb's truck and getting in. So much for sleeping tonight.

~

Macy still fumed as she turned into Brady's driveway. The nerve of that man. Why couldn't he get it through his thick skull she just wanted to be left alone? One thing goes wrong and he's right back in her life again. Granted, it had been less than a day, but what did it say about them, about her, that they couldn't even make it a day without interacting?

She and Hannah emerged from the car, taking their backpacks from the back seat. Macy locked the doors and followed Hannah up the walk to the front door. Brady took the steps in one stride, pulling his key ring from his pocket. Seb honked as he turned around and drove away.

"Why did you ride with him? Was he out here earlier?"

He glanced down at her as he twisted the key and let them inside. "I'll fill you in soon. Hannah, the spare room is still made up for you."

She nodded. "Good. I am ready for bed. Goodnight."

They echoed her words and watched her pad softly across the floor and disappear down the hallway. Macy walked into the kitchen and put her bag and keys on the counter, then opened a cabinet to get a glass down. Ice cubes clattered into it as she filled it from the dispenser in the fridge.

"Macy."

"What?" She switched the dispenser to water and pressed her glass to the lever, wishing it was that whiskey he had in the cupboard. Or wine. She could go for a glass of wine. "You want to answer my question now?"

He came to rest beside her, leaning a hip against the counter. "My brakes gave out on the way into town."

She choked on the drink she just took. Coughing, she looked up at him. "Holy crap. What happened?"

He shrugged. "I don't know yet. I had it towed back here. Our mechanic, Liam, will look at it tomorrow. I probably popped a line going over some rough terrain or something."

She raised an eyebrow and took another drink. "Well, I'm glad you're okay and didn't crash."

"Thanks, me too."

Silence filled the room, making prickles pop out on her skin as she tried to ignore the void between them. She finished her water while he stood there, then dumped out the ice and put the glass in the dishwasher. "I'm going to bed. Be careful on the mountain tomorrow," she said on her way to the door.

"Macy, wait."

Her heart rate kicked up a notch. God, would hearing her name from his lips ever not make her body feel funny things? She sucked in a breath and turned around.

Eyes locked on hers, he strode closer until he stood within touching range. All the fine hairs on her body stood on end at his proximity. She balled her hands into fists, but didn't back up. No need to remind him of the effect he had on her and give him the upper hand.

He wrapped one hand over the other, drumming his

fingers against his knuckles. "Look, I, um, I know this is not ideal, but I'm glad you're here, even if you aren't."

Guilt hit her hard. He was such a nice man, and she hated that she was causing him pain. "Brady—"

He held up a hand to stop her. "I don't want to argue. I just wanted you to know that. And I know you want me out of your life, but I'm not sure I can do that. I care about you. It's hard to just turn it off."

Macy held back a snort. He was preaching to the choir. "I care about you too."

He reached out and took a lock of her hair between his fingers, toying with the end. "Why can't we just be friends? Why can't we quash this crazy attraction?"

She drifted closer, unbidden. "I don't know. It would make life easier, wouldn't it?"

"Yeah." His feet shuffled toward her, bringing his chest within inches of hers.

His scent flooded her nose, sending shivers down her spine. "But I don't want to quash it. I want to make it grow." She took a step back. "And I know you don't."

He closed his eyes, his jaw working beneath his beard. When he opened them again, the look he gave her wasn't one she'd seen before. A spark of hope lit her chest, even as she did her damnedest to keep it at bay.

Her head tilted back as he stepped forward, stopping within inches again.

"What if I did?"

Her heart skipped. She swallowed, beating back the hope. "You know where I stand, Brady. I want a real shot at forever. Not just, let's see what happens."

He raised a hand and wove it into her hair on the side of her head, leaning down. "Nothing is guaranteed, but I just know I can't walk away from you. I know it's not what you want to hear, but right now, it's what I can give." His Adam's apple bobbed. "I'm trying, Macy."

Macy's mind whirled. Did she dare give him the chance he was asking for? Could she risk losing her heart completely—as well as months or years of her life—if she gave in and then he couldn't commit to her forever?

But if she didn't, would she always regret saying no? If she said yes, this was it. She couldn't see herself ever falling in love with anyone else if she let him past her defenses now. Was risking a lifetime alone worth giving him a chance now? Was it worth never knowing if she didn't?

Her heart pounded with a yearning to love this man. To be his everything and have him be hers. If she said no now, she would never get the chance.

She took his face in her hands, savoring the feel of his beard beneath her fingers. "I'm all in, Brady. Can you promise me you are too? That you'll give everything you have to make this work?"

His eyes searched hers. "You get all I can give. I'm working on making that everything."

The sincerity in his voice and on his face convinced her. She stood on her toes and kissed him.

Her feet left the ground as he bent at the knee and wrapped his arms around her waist, lifting her. He carried her from the room. Macy wrapped her legs around him. They reached his bedroom, and he kicked the door closed with his foot before setting her on her feet next to the bed.

She broke away to look up at him. Silence permeated the room, only cut by the sound of their harsh breathing. His hands roved down her back and over her hips.

"It was a bit presumptuous of me to bring you in here. You can go if you want." He stared at her, his hands stilling.

Macy ran her hands into his hair and tugged him down. "I'm right where I want to be."

He groaned and kissed her again, sending her body on red alert. It hadn't forgotten what it felt like to make love with him. She arched against him, wanting to be closer. He pulled away to rain soft kisses behind her ear and down her neck. Goosebumps broke out on Macy's skin and heat flooded her belly. His fingers burrowed beneath her top to stroke her bare back. She dug her fingers into his scalp, and he kissed her harder.

Through the haze now clouding her brain, she noted he'd turned on the small lamp on the nightstand and that they were moving. He lifted her and put her on the bed, taking her top off with deft hands.

"I didn't get a good look the first time." He straddled her thighs and looked down at her, his eyes tracing every line of her body. One hand grazed her collarbone with a featherlight touch, moving lower over the swells of her breasts and into the valley between.

Macy's nipples peaked beneath her bra, eager for his touch. She moaned and ran her hands up his muscular forearms.

"We're taking our time this time. Exhausted or not, I'm not rushing this. Not this time." He peeled down the cups of her bra, baring her breasts to tease the tips.

Another breathy moan escaped her. He bent his dark head to kiss her exposed flesh, working his way over the tops of her breasts to take the tip of one between his teeth. She let out a surprised shout, her hips bucking as he bit down, then soothed the bite with his tongue.

"Holy God." She gripped his thighs, her fingers digging into the muscles there as he moved to the other side. She felt him grin against her skin.

He moved away from her chest to kiss and lick his way down her stomach, tugging her leggings and panties down as he went. Every inch of skin he exposed, he laved attention on until Macy was a writhing mess of nerve-endings on the bed. When he reached her feet, he paused to look at her.

"Take off your bra."

She sat up, reaching behind her back for the hooks with shaking hands. After fumbling with it for several tries, she growled and spun it around to attack it from the front, finally freeing herself.

He chuckled, the sound a low rumble as he watched her. "I think that killed some of your arousal. I need to fix that." His eyes blazed in the soft glow of the lamp. Those large, working man's hands of his skated up her legs, pushing them apart as he went. He wrapped them around her hips, dipping his thumbs low over the tangle of auburn hair at the apex of her thighs.

When he slid over that little hidden nub, Macy's hips left the bed, and she let out a cry of pleasure. "More."

He slid two fingers through her folds, stroking her wet flesh. Macy panted as he worked her into a frenzy. She clutched the pillow under her head, needing something tangible to keep her from floating away as he slid one long digit inside her. When the second one joined the first, there was nothing that could keep her grounded. A climax ripped through her. She let out a high-pitched shriek, clamping her lips together as she remembered Hannah sleeping in the next room.

The mattress dipped as Brady moved. Macy was too sated to open her eyes. She knew he hadn't left because she could hear him moving. They popped open, though, when his weight—his naked weight—settled over her.

"I think I liked it better when you screamed." He smiled down at her.

She chuckled. "The next time there isn't a thirteen-year-old girl sleeping next door, I promise I'll make all the noise I can."

"I like the sound of that. I guess that means we need to go super slow this time. Draw it out." His head dipped to nip at the skin of her neck.

Macy's eyelids fluttered. *Damn.* "And you think that will make me *less* likely to scream?"

He smiled against her neck. "Probably not, but it'll sure be fun." He moved up and covered her mouth with his, preventing her from replying.

She got lost in a wash of sensation as he stroked and kissed and licked his way down her body again, sending her spiraling up the peak and over the edge once more. Macy was completely boneless when he came to rest between her legs, his erection teasing her entrance. More heat licked its way up her spine at the intimate touch.

He brushed the hair away from her face, staring down at her before he bent his head to place a tender kiss on her lips. Macy's heart soared at all the emotion behind it. He may not think he was ready to give her everything, but his heart was. She could feel it in his gentle touch.

Her thoughts fled as he pushed inside her, slow and steady, giving her time to adjust to him. Once he was fully seated, he pulled back to thrust forward again, just as slowly. Macy moaned. His pace stayed the same, driving her crazy.

"Faster," she growled.

"Nope. Slow, remember?"

She growled again, but it turned into a long moan as he sucked the tip of her breast into his mouth. Macy locked her ankles behind his back and thrust up, grinding against him as his slow pace inched her closer to the top.

"Brady." Breathless, she arched into him, her climax so close.

"Don't scream." He reached between them and teased her with his fingers.

Macy sailed over the top. She pressed a pillow to her face as a shout flew out of her mouth. It was impossible to hold it in as her body shattered. Exquisite pleasure flowed through her, burning her from the inside out.

Brady groaned, picking up his pace. Macy's bonelessness faded, his thrusts ramping her up again. Her flesh was so sensitive, she was at the top in moments, flying into the ether with him this time. His mouth covered hers, swallowing her scream. Together, they rode the white-hot waves until they went limp.

She let herself melt into the mattress, his weight a warm blanket. When he rolled away, she protested.

"I'll crush you if I don't move." He flopped next to her and pulled the comforter and sheet from under them to cover their bodies.

Macy rolled into him, tangling her fingers in the dark whirl of hair on his chest. He covered her hand with his. She felt him relax as he took a deep breath. The words "I love you" stuck in her throat. She wanted so badly to shout it from the top of the mountain, but she knew it was too soon for him.

So, she snuggled closer and closed her eyes, praying one day soon, she could say it and have him say it back.

Sixteen

Snowflakes drifted from the steel gray sky as Brady rode alongside Seb into the mountains in search of the cave. He shifted his balaclava higher on his face under his helmet to cover his nose, which felt like a popsicle after riding at speed for the last couple of hours. They'd slowed as the terrain steepened, so the bite wasn't as bad, but he was ready to be out of the wind. Winter still had a grip at this elevation, even though it was spring.

He thought back to that morning, hoping the memory of Macy's naked body pressed to his would chase away the chill. It did, but it also left him uncomfortable. Being aroused and riding through rough terrain was not pleasant. But now that the image was there, he couldn't chase it away, and despite his discomfort, he didn't want to.

Something snapped in him last night. Seb's advice had already been swirling around his brain when the call about the break-in came in. His only thought was getting to her and making sure she was safe. It helped him realize he couldn't disappear from her life. If that meant he needed to set some of his reservations aside, then he needed to change. He couldn't imagine life without Macy. The more he thought about her, about her role in his life, he knew friendship wasn't all they were meant to have. It took him long enough to figure that out—he was still struggling with it, but he was trying. Overcoming years of putting up walls and steering clear of relationships wouldn't be easy. But he couldn't lose her because he was afraid.

The growl of their ATVs echoed through the trees as they climbed, the engines changing pitch as they worked harder to get up the steeper slope. They crested the ridge and Brady signaled everyone to stop.

"We're close. I came up here to see where we were. The cave is that way." He pointed forward to the left.

"Lead the way." Seb motioned him on.

Brady put the ATV in gear and took off over the ridge toward the cliff, slowing once they were close to where he thought they climbed up. He rolled forward along the edge, looking for the stand of trees he'd anchored the rope to.

"There." He stopped and pointed to some trees. "This is the spot." He shut off his ATV and climbed off, removing his helmet and tugging his balaclava down as he walked toward the edge. He could just make out the ledge at the cave entrance from where he stood.

Seb came to stand next to him.

"Down there."

He glanced down. "It's a good thing our M.E. and forensic scientist are experienced climbers. Could you imagine doing this with the M.E. from Colorado Springs?"

Brady grinned. He'd met Dr. Caulfield a couple times. The guy was nice, but he was in his sixties and overweight. "We'd have to rig up some kind of chair. Or bring the body to him."

"I think I'd prefer the latter. We have to do that anyway.

Let's get our ropes set up and get down there. If we're lucky, we can get out of here and back to civilization by dark."

That would be ideal. He had no desire to spend the night out here again.

Alex walked up beside them, carrying two harnesses. He held them out. "Put these on. Katie's working on securing a rope."

Brady took the harness and stepped into it, fastening it around his waist and making sure the straps were tight.

"Who's going first?" Alex asked.

"I will. I've been down there, so I can help guide everyone else in."

"Sounds good." He handed Brady the rope. "You get down there and we'll start lowering equipment to you."

Brady tied himself off, then stepped over the side, walking down the cliff face to the ledge below. The harness and belay system made it a lot easier than the last time he did this. His feet touched down, and he unhooked himself.

"I'm down," he yelled up the cliff. Seb appeared at the top and gave him a thumbs up.

He leaned out of the cave, watching for the supply bags. The first one soon appeared. He snagged it as it swung in front of the cave entrance, and he pulled it inside. Several more followed, along with a rescue basket to put the body bag in. He brought everything inside and lined it up against the wall, out of the way.

Rocks bouncing down signaled an incoming climber. Brady looked out to see Seb coming his way. He helped his brother inside, where he unclipped from the rope so Katie could come down next. Within a few minutes, she, Alex, and Katie's assistant, Emma, joined them.

"You guys spent the night in here?" Katie shuddered. "How big were the spiders?"

"I didn't notice. We were too busy trying to warm up."

She tipped her head. "True. So, where's this body?"

"Back there." He pointed into the darkness.

"Okay. Everybody grab some equipment and let's go," Seb said.

Brady hefted a bag and led the way into the cave to the area where it narrowed.

"Good God, I have to crawl in there?" Katie said. She glanced at Emma. "You ready for this?"

"No, but let's just get it done. I hope my butt's not too big."

"Hannah fit, and she's as tall as either of you," Brady said.

"Yeah, but I'm betting she doesn't have this ass." Emma poked herself in the butt. The woman was curvy, but not overly so.

"We're gonna find out. Come on, Em." Katie dropped to her knees, flashlight in hand, pushing a bag full of evidence collection equipment ahead of her. Emma dropped down behind her with her camera case. The two women shimmied their way through the passage to the other side.

"You know, it looks like part of this caved in," Katie said as she worked her way into the narrow space. "There's loose rock on one side."

Alex, Brady, and Seb crouched to look through the tunnel. Brady hadn't noticed that before, but she was right. One side was filled in with boulders and small rocks while the other was the smooth face of the cave walls.

"Wow. It's a lot bigger in here than I thought it would be. We're lucky nothing's made this a den. Though, there have been some little critters in here. There are bits of torn food wrappers mixed with animal fur." Katie said as she emerged from the passageway into the cavern beyond and looked around.

"This cave is probably too high for much of anything to get in," Seb said.

"True. Okay, Em, start taking pictures while I get my stuff out."

The other woman snapped a series of photographs of the body and the area around it, then moved further into the cavern.

"There's another passage back here."

Brady frowned. The girls hadn't mentioned that.

"What?" Seb leaned closer. "Can you fit inside?"

"Yeah, it's bigger. Hang on."

They waited while Emma explored.

"Honey, what can you tell me about the body?" Alex said.

Katie crouched to look through the passageway. "I'd say it's an adolescent male, eleven to thirteen." She shone her light at the ground around the body. "There's some hair here."

"Still?"

"Yeah. It's dark, but from the look of it and where it is, I'd say it belongs to our victim. I'll make sure Emma photographs it up close before I collect it."

"Do you think you can get DNA from it?" Seb asked.

"Maybe. But that's a big maybe. There probably isn't a root ball left on any of these strands. I might be able to get some mitochondrial DNA, but that will only do us any good if we have someone to match it to who's willing to give us a sample."

"If it's who I think it is, we should be able to get DNA from him. Both kinds," Seb said.

"I'll do what I can."

"Who do you think it is?" Brady asked.

"Robbie Knight's older brother, Steven. He disappeared almost forty years ago at the age of twelve."

Brady frowned. "I didn't know Robbie had a brother."

"Me either. Kerr told me. Apparently, he and Robbie were best friends as children."

"Seriously? That's an unlikely pair."

"Now, yes. I looked more into Robbie's background. His family was upper middle class. His dad was a finance officer for the bank. Kerr said Robbie fell in with a bad crowd and never got out."

The sound of footsteps in the dirt as Emma came running back brought their conversation to a halt. She held up a backpack. "I found this back there. And yes, I took pictures first." She set it on the ground in front of Katie, then raised her camera.

Katie unzipped the bag, and Emma snapped an image of what was inside.

"What do you see?" Brady asked.

"Clothes, mostly." Katie held up a shirt. Emma took a picture, then Katie put it in an evidence bag. They went through the pack, an article of clothing at a time.

"You think the kid was running away?" Brady asked Seb.

"That was the consensus when he disappeared. He took a backpack with him and some clothes."

"Have you talked to Robbie?"

Seb nodded. "I tried. He was blitzed when I went to his trailer yesterday morning. As soon as I mentioned you found who I thought was Steven, he asked where he was, then slammed the door in my face. Wouldn't come out again, no matter how hard I tried. I've been keeping an eye out around town and so have my deputies, but he hasn't shown up yet."

"You'd think he'd want to help." Alex said.

Seb shrugged. "From what Kerr said, the family was never the same after Steven disappeared. The dad stayed at work late all the time, and their mom turned to alcohol. They're both long dead."

"So, we need Robbie to confirm an ID," Alex said.

"Most likely, yes. Unless there's something on the body that will tell me definitively it's Steven Knight."

~

Cold seeped into Brady's ass from the hard ground. Katie and Emma had been in the cavern for over an hour now. He, Seb, and Alex literally sat around waiting while they processed the scene. He glanced toward the passageway again, hoping they would be done soon.

Katie's shout that they were coming out was an answer to his prayer. He scrambled to his feet.

"Thank God," Alex said. "My ass is numb."

"How?" Seb asked. "You were up walking them through how to bag the skeleton."

"Not the whole time. That ground is hard."

"Try sleeping on it," Brady said, standing.

Emma emerged, holding a rope. She passed it to Brady while Seb and Alex helped her to her feet. Brady reeled in the nylon, pulling the body bag free of the tunnel. Katie emerged behind it with her own tow rope attached to her equipment. Alex helped her up while Seb took the rope.

"Did you look at the body yet?" she asked Alex.

"It just came out of the tunnel, babe."

She waved a hand. "Slacker." With a grin, she walked over to the body bag and unzipped it. Alex dropped down next to her.

Seb and Brady stood over them, looking at the jumble of bones they revealed. Brady didn't know how they saw anything in that mess. It was like a jigsaw puzzle to him.

"It's definitely male, and Katie's age projection looks spot on. We still need to have the remains examined by a forensic anthropologist, but that gives you a good place to start, Seb. I'll call the university when we return and get the new guy they hired down here to look at our victim."

"Can we trust him?" Seb asked.

"I think so. He's from out of state. Vermont. And he's a

newly minted Ph.D. He hasn't had time to be sucked into any of Dr. White's circles." Alex frowned. "Hey, what's that?" He pointed to a vertebra. "Babe, I need some gloves."

Katie dug into her kit and handed him a pair. He put them on, then lifted the bone from the bag.

"What do you see?" Katie asked.

He pointed to an area on the rounded inside of the bone. "See that knick?"

"Oh my God," Katie said as she leaned closer and got a better look.

"What?" Seb asked.

"Your victim was stabbed," Alex said.

"Who would stab an eleven-year-old?" Brady mused. "Scratch that. We've seen plenty of deviants lately. Hell, what's one more? Jesus."

"Great. A forty-year-old murder case." Seb pinched the bridge of his nose. "I guess Robbie's going to talk to me whether he wants to or not now. Let's get packed up and get out of here."

Alex closed the body bag. Brady picked up the forensic equipment and headed for the entrance. Seb didn't have to tell him twice. He was ready to go home.

"I'll go up first." He attached the rope to his harness. "You guys can toss a coin for who comes next."

"I will," Seb said. "I learned a long time ago not to touch Katie's stuff unless she said to."

Katie grinned. "Smart man. You two go. Emma will follow you, then Alex and I will send everything up and follow it."

"Sounds good," Seb said. He glanced at Brady. "Be careful."

"This is easy compared to last time." He gave his brother a half smile and stepped to the edge of the ledge. "See you topside." He slid his ascender up the rope, then down, and his feet left the ground.

Using the device as well as climbing up the rock face, Brady made good time to the top. He cleared the edge and hollered down for Seb to start his climb. When Seb's dark hair appeared at the top, he reached down to help him over the edge.

Emma came next, flying up the rope to Brady's surprise. The woman was much more athletic than she looked. Once she was standing on the cliff, he hollered down for Alex to send up the rescue basket. Because the skeleton didn't take up much space, they were able to pack all the equipment on the sled with the body bag. Brady pulled up the rope they used to lower the stuff. Emma and Seb grabbed the basket as it reached the top, helping it over the edge.

Cold wind blew down Brady's neck. He tugged his balaclava up over his head with a scowl. "Tell them to get their asses up here so we can—" His words died in his throat as a searing pain ripped through his chest.

"Brady!" Seb's shout sounded far away to Brady's ears.

The crack of a rifle echoed through the wilderness as he fell to his knees. He put a hand to his chest, feeling a sticky wetness seeping through his layers of clothing. What the hell?

"Shit!" Seb skidded to a halt on his knees in front of Brady. "Someone's shooting at us. Emma! Get behind those trees."

Brady looked at Seb. It was hard to breathe. "Seb?"

"Don't talk. Conserve your air." Another shot pinged off the ground behind Seb. "Goddammit! We need to get out of the open."

"Were those gunshots?" Alex's voice carried up from below.

"Yes! Brady's been shot. Stay down there!" Seb stood, hurrying around to hook his arms under Brady's so he could drag him across the ground to the cluster of trees where Emma took shelter. A third shot hit a tree trunk just past Seb's head.

"Fuck, that was close!"

"Who's shooting at us?" Emma said.

"No idea. But it's not my first concern right now. We need to stop the bleeding. Where's the forensics bag?"

She pointed past the trees. It was still in the sled with the body.

"There's—first aid—" Brady pointed at his ATV, unable to get more out as he struggled to breathe. His chest was on fire, but his hands were numb. A ringing in his ears threatened to drown out everything else.

Seb and Emma turned to look at the vehicle.

"Stay with him. Put some pressure on the wound." Seb stood and ran toward the ATV, sliding behind it as a bullet pinged off the bumper.

Brady closed his eyes and concentrated on inhaling enough air. His chest gurgled with every breath and his teeth chattered as cold seeped in. Pressure on his chest made him moan.

"I'm sorry," Emma whispered.

"It's—okay." He gritted his teeth against the pain, fighting the blackness crowding the edges of his vision.

Seb returned, first aid kit in hand. He unzipped it, finding gauze. Brady barely noticed him ripping open the packages. The pressure on his chest eased for a moment, but cold air replaced it as Seb tore his coat and shirt open to press the gauze against the wound. He hissed as Seb bore down, putting his weight behind it.

"Emma, hold this. I need to call for help."

Brady said a prayer of thanks for the sat phone none of them left home without anymore. He opened his eyes, seeing Seb move away to get the phone. His breath rattled and his vision narrowed further. He was fighting a losing battle with consciousness.

Commotion from the other side of the trees helped him

beat back the darkness. Alex's face loomed over him a moment later.

"I told you to stay down there," Seb growled.

"Yeah, screw that." He moved Emma's hands away to look at Brady's wound, then replaced the pressure.

Brady moaned. "Stop doing that," he bit out. "Leave it."

"Sorry, man. Is there an exit wound?"

"Not that we noticed, but we didn't really look," Emma said.

"I need to roll you over, Brady." Alex didn't wait for him to respond. "Katie, help me."

Hands pushed and pulled him, rolling him to his side. His head swam as the darkness now consumed all but a pinpoint of his vision.

"Chopper's on the way," Seb said. "How's he doing?"

"Not good. There's no exit wound. With the location, I'm worried about his liver as well as his lung."

Brady stared up at them. He could just make out their faces now and barely make out their words. Everything was muffled, like he had cotton in his ears. His eyelids fluttered. Macy's mischievous smile and lively blue eyes flashed in his mind. His heart lurched as the thought hit him that he might not see her again. That he left things unfinished. She deserved better. He raised a hand and touched Seb's arm.

"Seb. Tell—" He swallowed, fighting to stay awake. "Tell Mace—I'm—sorry. And I—love her."

"You can tell her yourself." Seb's voice broke. "You fight, you hear me? Don't make me tell Macy you died. Please."

Brady tried to keep his eyes open, but he was so tired. His head swam and the pain in his chest faded, replaced by a heavy nothingness. He was numb. Everywhere. Fatigue tugged at his limbs, weighing them down like he was a hundred feet underwater. His vision went dark as he succumbed to the pull.

Seventeen

The bell over the door jingled, and Macy looked up from making a latte to see Jace walk in.

"Hi!" She looked back at her task. "Did you bring more baby pictures for me to fawn over?"

"Macy."

The quiet, serious tone of his voice made her hands still. She looked at him, noting the grim set to his handsome features. Her heart lurched, then its tempo quickened.

"What happened?"

"They were ambushed bringing the remains out of the cave. Brady was shot. He's being life-flighted to Denver."

The cup in her hand slid from her fingers, the hot liquid splashing all over the floor and her shoes. She barely noticed. Her knees buckled, and she sagged into the counter. Anna, the woman working with her, caught her around the waist, holding her up while Jace raced around to help.

"He can't die," she whispered, staring at him. A lone tear tracked down her face.

Jace's jaw worked. "I know. Come on. I'm driving you to Denver."

She nodded and glanced at Anna.

"Go. I'll mind the café. I can even stay over today."

"Thank you."

"Of course. Call me later with an update, okay?"

Macy nodded and let Jace lead her around the counter and out the door. As he helped her into his truck, Anna came running out the door with her purse.

"You might need this."

"Thanks."

"Yep. I hope he's okay."

With a strained smile, Macy shut the door. Anna backed away as Jace got in the driver's seat and started the truck, pulling away from the curb.

Macy clenched her hands around the strap of her purse, smoothing her thumbs over the leather. Her mind whirled with questions, but the one that stood out was about everyone else.

"Are the others okay?"

"Yes. I sent Gentry and Wilder to provide cover fire in the chopper going to pick up Brady. They didn't see anyone. Whoever shot him must have left when they heard the helicopter. Alex went with him to Denver, while the deputies stayed with the others to help them make it safely down the mountain to Benson. Seb's been calling dispatch every fifteen minutes to report their progress, and they're keeping me informed."

"Why him? Why not Seb?" She held up a hand. "That came out wrong."

"I understand what you mean. And we don't know why it was Brady. Maybe the shooter was trying to take them all out and Brady was the easiest target. Seb said there were several more shots, and they were all long range."

She said a prayer of thanks no one else was hurt. "How bad is it? And don't sugarcoat it."

"It's bad. The bullet went in on the right side of his chest near his diaphragm. Seb said he has a collapsed lung at the very least. They weren't sure about damage to other organs, though, when I talked to him. He was unconscious when they loaded him into the chopper."

Macy closed her eyes as tears trailed down her cheeks. She prayed he would still be alive when they reached the hospital. *Please, God, don't let him die.* She didn't know what she would do if she lost him.

Jace's hand covered hers. "Have some faith? He's tough."

"I know," she whispered. "I'm trying."

He squeezed her hand.

Macy leaned her head against the window, doing her best to keep it together. She couldn't break down yet. Things were still too uncertain for her to let the tears take over. What good would it do for her to cry over something that might not be as serious as it sounded? What if he was awake and sitting up, talking when they reached the hospital? She would have cried for nothing.

She sniffed, feeling calmer even though she knew she was probably deluding herself. But if she wanted to stay sane, that was what she was going with.

The ride passed in a blur. She remembered little of the drive and only came back to herself when she noticed the signs for the emergency department as Jace entered the hospital complex. He parked the car, then they jogged in together. At the registration desk, all the girl working could tell them was that he was in surgery and directed them toward the waiting room.

Feeling defeated, Macy followed Jace down the hallway to the surgery center. He pushed the door open, holding it for her.

"Macy. Jace."

She turned at the sound of her name. Alex rose from his seat by the window. She hurried over to him.

"How is he? What did they say about his injuries? Is he going to be all right?"

Alex put a hand on her shoulder. "Let's have a seat?" He motioned to a set of couches toward the back of the room, then led them over.

She perched on the edge of one. "Please, Alex. I need to know how he's doing." Jace sat next to her, offering moral support.

"He's alive. They pumped a couple units of blood into him when we arrived and took him straight to surgery. The surgeon promised regular updates, and the first one came about half an hour ago. The bullet tore through his right lung, bounced off the metal plate on his ribcage, then back through the lung to rest near his spine. It missed his heart by millimeters. The nurse I spoke to said he's going to lose the lower lobe of his right lung."

Macy sucked in a breath and covered her mouth with both hands. More tears filled her eyes. "And after that? Is he going to be okay?"

"His prognosis is guarded. He lost a lot of blood. If his body can survive the shock of that as well as the surgery, he should be fine. The next twenty-four hours are critical."

She leaned her elbows on her knees and ran her hands over her face. "Oh my God," she muttered under her breath.

Alex laid a hand on her shoulder again. "Brady's a strong, healthy man, Macy. And he's a fighter. He'll make it."

She nodded. He had to. Life without him wasn't worth a lick. If he lived through this, she vowed to love him enough for both of them. She just wanted him in her life.

A nudge to her arm brought Macy out of the light doze she was in. She sat up, yawning as she looked at Alex. He pointed to a man in blue scrubs striding toward them.

"That's Brady's surgeon."

Any traces of sleep vanished. Macy stood, waiting for the doctor to reach her.

"Dr. Walsh." Alex held out a hand.

"Dr. Randall. Is this Mr. Archer's family?"

"His girlfriend, Macy, and his brother-in-law, Jace. The rest of his family stayed behind so we didn't overrun the hospital."

Walsh's eyes widened. "How many are there?"

"A lot," Jace said. "How is he?"

"He's stable for now. I removed the lower lobe of his right lung and stitched up a hole in his liver. The bullet nicked the top of it as it passed through the lung. So long as there aren't any complications, he should be fine with time."

Macy's knees went weak as relief filled her. Tears of a different variety threatened to fall. "Can we see him?"

"Yes. I wanted to make sure he was settled in recovery before I came to talk to you. They should transfer him to the ICU soon. If you'll follow me, I'll take you up there to wait."

She resisted the urge to run to the elevator. She needed to see him and reassure herself he was okay. Her foot tapped the linoleum floor as they rode the car to the fourth floor. Couldn't this thing go any faster?

The doors parted on a ding, and she followed Dr. Walsh onto the floor. He led them to the waiting room, where a volunteer behind a desk greeted them.

"These people are waiting on Brady Archer to arrive from surgery," he said to the older woman.

She smiled and nodded. "I'll let the nursing staff know his family is here." She picked up the phone.

"I'm sure it won't be long. If you have any questions, let the nurses know and they'll contact me."

They thanked the doctor and he left. Macy paced to the window, staring out at the dark sky. Clouds obscured the moon and stars, making the world outside feel closed in. It matched her mood. If they didn't bring him up here soon so she could see him, she would go stir-crazy.

Minutes ticked by in slow-motion until finally the phone rang. Macy spun around to stare at the older woman whose nametag read "Marsha," willing it to be someone telling her they could see Brady.

Marsha hung up and smiled at her, rising from her chair. "That was the nurse's station. Follow me and I'll take you to his room." The woman picked up a cane hanging off the back of her chair and hobbled toward the door.

A scream built in Macy's throat. She clamped her lips together to keep it in.

"Ma'am, why don't you just tell us his room number and we'll show ourselves. No need for you to walk all that way," Jace said.

Macy wanted to kiss him.

"Oh, it's no trouble. I need to stretch my legs, anyway."

Dammit! Macy blew out a harsh breath through her nose and followed the elderly woman from the room. She glanced at Jace as they trudged along. He shrugged, and she sighed. He'd tried, and for that she was thankful.

"Okay, here we go." Marsha stopped outside a door, smiling at them.

Macy thanked her and pushed through the door, not waiting on Jace and Alex. She stopped just over the threshold as she got her first glimpse of him. He was pale and tubes and wires were everywhere; coming off his wrist, attached to his exposed chest, and snaking out from under the bedsheet covering his lower half.

Her lower lip wobbled, and she sucked it in to hold back the sob. Hands shaking, she walked to his bedside and leaned over him, brushing a lock of hair away from his forehead. She pressed a kiss to his temple.

His eyelids fluttered, and he turned his head toward her.

"Brady?" She couldn't hold back the smile when he opened his eyes, revealing their dark depths.

"Macy?"

"Yeah. Hey." She combed her fingers through his hair. "Do you remember what happened?"

"Sort of. Fiery pain and the crack of a rifle. And blood." He closed his eyes for a moment, swallowing hard. "Where am I?"

"Denver. Seb called in a medevac and they life-flighted you here. You lost the lower lobe of your right lung and have some damage to your liver, but you should be okay."

A tear rolled down his face. "I'm so sorry, Macy."

"For what? You didn't mean to get shot."

"No. For all the time I wasted. You were right to cut me out of your life. I'm an idiot."

She smiled. "I've known that a long time." She sniffed, happy he was awake and himself, even if he was ready to fall asleep again. She leaned down and kissed his forehead. "Get some rest and we'll talk later." She straightened to move away, but he snagged her hand with surprising strength. Her brow dipped as their eyes met.

"I love you. I'm sorry it took this to get me to see it."

Macy's heart stalled, then kicked into overdrive, the pace making her dizzy. She squeezed his hand. Emotion made her voice thick as she replied. "I love you too, you crazy man." She bent and pressed a soft kiss to his lips. "Get some sleep."

He nodded, his eyes already closing. "So long as you're here when I wake up."

"No place I'd rather be."

Eighteen

Macy sank onto the couch under the window in Brady's room, curling up under the blanket the nurses brought her to ward off the chill in the room. It was night two in the hospital and she was as tired as Brady. Today was full of physical therapy and visitors. Most of his family, including the twins, were by to see him. But the lights in the corridor were low now, and the floor was quiet.

A glance outside revealed a bright moon. Macy couldn't wait until they were home again so she could see the stars too. They were washed out here in the city with all the bright lights. With a sigh, she brought her phone up to call Seb. It was late, but she needed to know how things were going. He and Jace hadn't visited today, and the others knew little about the investigation.

The phone rang several times before a tired sounding Sebastian picked up.

"Macy? Is everything okay?"

"Everything's fine." She kept her voice low so as not to wake Brady. "He's sleeping. I just wanted to know what was happening there. Are you any closer to figuring out who shot him and why?"

He sighed. She could hear the disgust in it.

"Not really. I can't find Robbie Knight anywhere. No one's seen him since the day before yesterday. And get this. Daniel Kerr is missing."

"What? Did you call Denise and ask if she's heard from him?"

"Yep. She hasn't since yesterday morning. He called to check on Jessie, but didn't say anything about what he was up to. She's tried calling him several times, but it just rolls to voicemail."

"You don't think—" The D.A. couldn't possibly be the one who pulled the trigger. Could he?

"I don't know what to think. Nothing would surprise me, though. Not after the string of bad luck we've had this year."

It wouldn't her, either. If the past ten months had taught her anything, it was that nothing was impossible, even the worst things imaginable.

"I'm trying to keep an open mind, though. He and Robbie were friends once. Maybe he's out looking for him, too."

"Without telling anyone?"

"Maybe he's protecting him."

"From what?

"The shooter. Himself. Me. I don't know." He yawned. "I'm going to keep looking, though. For both of them. In the morning."

She chuckled. "Yeah, okay, I get the hint. Get some sleep, I'll talk to you later."

"Goodnight, Macy."

"Goodnight." She hung up the phone, resting her chin on it for a moment as she thought about their conversation. She couldn't picture Dan as a killer. Robbie either, for that matter, but she didn't know him that well. He was a drunk, but he was never violent.

A yawn overtook her. She should have changed into the pajamas London and Tara brought for her before she settled on the couch. For a brief moment, she contemplated sleeping in the clothes she had on, but knew the flannel pants, thick socks and long-sleeved t-shirt would be much more comfortable than her skinny jeans and cardigan.

She pushed the blanket off and stood up, picking up the tote her friends brought before exiting the room to use the family restroom down the hall. She'd take a quick shower, then put on her pajamas.

In the restroom, she dug out the travel toiletries stuffed at the bottom and stripped out of her clothes, hopping into the shower stall. The warm water flowed over her tired body, easing some of the stress from today, relaxing her. She soaped her hair and body, then rinsed off and stepped out. The hospital's towels were scratchy and too small, but they did their job. She wiped the water from herself and tugged on a sports bra and her top, then wrapped another towel around her hair to suck out some of the moisture while she finished dressing and brushed her teeth. After combing out her thick hair, she gathered her things and walked back down the hall to Brady's room.

Tiptoeing over the threshold, she moved to the opposite side of the room from his bed to stow her bag. The hair on the back of her neck stood up a split second before a hand went over her mouth and an arm around her waist.

"Don't scream."

Whiskey-soured breath wafted past her nose. Fear rose in her throat, choking off her airway. She gagged behind the man's hand and tried to suck in a breath through her nose. Body rigid, she dug her nails into the arm holding her tight.

"I'll let you go, just don't scream, okay?" The voice

softened.

She nodded, her mind clearing a bit at the less threatening tone. He let go of her mouth. Macy sucked in a lung full of air. The arm around her waist tensed, then relaxed when she didn't scream. He let her go, and she spun around. Her eyes grew wide as she recognized the man in gray janitorial scrubs and ball cap.

"Robbie. What are you doing here? How did you get in?"

He swallowed hard, his eyes leaving hers to look outside before coming back. "The nurses thought I was part of the cleaning staff. I'm sorry."

"You're sorry? For lying?" A thought hit her. "Wait. Are you the one who shot Brady?"

He nodded, his eyes leaving hers again to stare at a point past her shoulder. "And loosened his brake lines and wrote that message on your wall. When it didn't stop you, I followed them into the mountains." A tear rolled down his face. "I saw them bring Steven's body over the edge and I just couldn't let them take him out of there."

"Why do all of that? Don't you want him to be buried with your parents? To know what happened to him?"

"I know what happened to him."

The certainty in his voice sent shivers down her spine. She swallowed, watching him carefully. "What happened to him, Robbie?"

"I stabbed him." His brow furrowed and his fists clenched. "I had to."

"You killed your brother? When you were a child?" Her question ended on a whisper.

He nodded. "Steven was evil. I had to."

Steven was the evil one? "What did he do?"

"He liked to torture animals. Frogs, squirrels, kittens. He strangled my puppy and made me watch. Said it was because the puppy was bad. He wouldn't stop peeing in the house.

Steven didn't like it. He told me if I told Mom and Dad he would do the same to me while I slept."

Movement behind him drew her attention. She schooled her face, hoping she kept it emotionless so Robbie wouldn't turn around and see Brady sitting up.

"Is that why you stabbed him?" she asked, trying to keep him focused on her. Brady flipped the blankets off and lowered his legs over the side of the bed.

He shook his head. "No. That came later. We were camping. He wanted to go find some night critters."

Macy held up a hand. "Wait. I thought he disappeared from your house."

Robbie shook his head. "That's what Mom and Dad wanted people to think." His shoulders slumped. "I had to."

"Start at the beginning. I want to understand." She flicked her eyes past him. Brady was out of bed, standing next to it with his gaze locked on Robbie as he clutched the guardrail.

"He woke me up and said we were going hunting. I didn't want to go, but I knew if I didn't, he'd find a way to hurt me. We put our shoes on, and he picked up Dad's hunting knife, then we snuck out."

Brady had a hold of his IV pole now, using it like a cane. Macy tried to signal him with a hand down by her hip. She wanted to hear Robbie's story before he intervened. To understand why. Brady must have seen her, because he paused at the end of the bed.

"I was smaller than Steven, so I had trouble keeping up. I tripped and scared away the raccoon he was after. He turned on me. Came at me with that knife and said if he couldn't hunt critters, he'd just hunt me. I got to my feet and ran. I knew if he caught me, he'd kill me. Somehow, I got way ahead of him, so I climbed a tree. I must have made a noise, because he found me. When he tried to climb up to get me, I jumped down, but I wasn't quick enough. He jumped down after me, but he dropped his knife. I picked it up and didn't think. I just stabbed him when he came at me again."

Macy sucked in a breath, her heart breaking for the young boy put in such a terrible situation.

"How did he end up in the cave?"

"I ran back to the tent and woke up my parents. Dad told us he would take care of it. I didn't know what he did with Steven's body until you found him. I just knew he was out there in the forest. We went home that night, and Mom and Dad made up a story about how we came home early because I wasn't feeling well, which upset Steven and he ran away. We lived close enough to the edge of town, it wasn't hard to get people to think he got lost in the woods." Tears trickled over his eyelids to trail down his face. "Why couldn't you just leave him there?" he asked, his voice a rough whisper. "He was a monster. Now he's back."

"Back? No, Robbie, he's still dead. Nothing but bones that can't hurt you ever again."

"No." He grabbed the sides of his head. "No, no, no, no! He's out there, waiting for me. And it's *your* fault!" He tossed his hands away and took a step toward Macy.

She held up her hands and moved back. Brady lurched away from the bed.

"Hey!"

Robbie spun around to see Brady advancing on him.

"You want to blame someone, blame me. I led the police to him. I pulled him up that cliff. Macy had nothing to do with it." He stood straight, trying to make the smaller man think twice about taking him on, but Macy could see the pain on his face he tried to hide.

She ran around to stand between them. She couldn't let Robbie attack him. Brady was in no state to defend himself against someone blinded by fear. "Robbie, please. No one needs to get hurt. I know you think Steven's free to hurt you again, but that's just not the case. Let's have a seat, okay?" She held out a hand toward him, motioning him toward the couch. He drifted that direction. "We can talk about this, then we'll call Seb and you can tell him what happened."

Robbie froze.

Crap! She pushed it too far, mentioning the police.

"No." He backed away. "I'm not going to jail. Not for murder. I don't care that I killed Steven. He deserved to die. He was evil."

"Seb's not going to arrest you for murder. He'll hear your story and understand. You were a child, scared your brother would kill you if you didn't do something." And as for shooting Brady and all the other things he did, she was fairly certain a judge would see grounds for insanity. The poor man had some serious mental issues when it came to his brother. "Please. Let's just sit. Everything will be okay, all right?"

He stared at her for several moments before his face crumpled, and the tears began in earnest. "I'm so sorry. I didn't mean for anyone to get hurt. I just wanted to keep Steven buried so he couldn't hurt me anymore."

Macy shushed him softly and guided him toward the couch. "It's okay. We understand." She helped him sit, leaving a hand on his shoulder for a moment before stepping back and letting him cry.

She moved to Brady's side. "You okay?" Sweat dotted his brow.

"Yeah." His knees buckled.

"Whoa!" She wrapped an arm around his waist and braced her feet to stay upright as she took on his weight. Staggering under her load, she helped him back to the bed. He sank down with a wince and a groan.

"Are you sure you're all right?" She laid her hands on his shoulders.

He nodded, his breath hitching with pain. "Yeah. Just...

need a second."

Macy looked away from him to check on Robbie, who still sobbed on the couch, and a thought occurred to her. She walked over to crouch in front of him. "Robbie." He continued to cry. "Robbie, look at me." She touched his knee. He hiccupped, but looked at her. "Where's Dan? Have you seen him?"

"Dan?" The tears slowed.

She nodded. "Daniel Kerr. No one's heard from him lately. Do you know where he is?"

His face crumpled, and his shoulders sagged. "He's in the shed at my house."

Macy swallowed hard, afraid to ask her next question, but knowing she had to. "Is he okay?"

Robbie shrugged. "He came to me and asked what I knew. He figured it all out. I had to stop him from telling. To keep Steven away."

"Robbie, did you kill Dan?"

"No." He shook his head hard. "No. He was alive when I put him in the shed. I could never kill Danny. He's my friend."

Macy's shoulders dropped. *Thank God*. She patted Robbie on the knee. "Good. Thank you for telling me. I'll make sure he's safe."

Tears welled in Robbie's eyes again. "I'm sorry. I didn't want to hurt anyone. I just wanted Steven to leave me alone."

"I know. And he will. I promise. Steven can't hurt anyone ever again."

He sniffed and hugged himself, sinking into the couch.

Macy stood and backed toward the door, keeping her eyes on him as she opened it. He didn't move, just stared off into space as silent tears coursed down his cheeks. She stepped out of the room and got the nurse's attention at the desk.

"Call security. Brady's shooter is in the room."

The woman's eyes widened.

"Everything is fine," she hastened to assure her. "There's no danger. He's mentally ill and is crying on the couch. Just get them up here. I'll call the sheriff."

The nurse nodded and picked up the phone. Macy ducked back inside and found her phone to call Seb.

Within twenty minutes, chaos swamped the small room. Macy sat in a chair near the head of Brady's bed and watched one of Seb's deputies lead a subdued Robbie from the room in handcuffs. Seb stopped at the end of the bed, watching as they left before looking at Macy and Brady.

"You doing okay?" He arched an eyebrow at his brother.

Brady nodded, eyelids drooping. The nurses gave him something for pain after they called security, and he'd been fighting to stay awake since. "I'm good. Glad it's over."

Seb's mouth pulled down. "Yeah."

"Why are you frowning?" Macy asked.

Seb shrugged and crossed his arms. "It's just sad. All those lives ruined because of one evil soul."

"It could have been more. If Steven hadn't died as a child, he could have been another Ryan Marsters."

"True." Seb straightened. "Do you need anything?"

Macy glanced at Brady, then shook her head. "No. He's practically asleep and I'm going to bed as soon as you all clear out of here."

"Okay." He tapped Brady's foot. "Stay out of trouble, yeah? No more late-night phone calls that send me rushing from my bed."

Brady's mouth quirked. "I'll try. I am marrying Macy, though, so no guarantees."

Her head whipped around to stare at him, open-mouthed. A smile quirked his beautiful lips. "What?"

"And on that note, I'm out. I'll see you tomorrow." Seb's boots thudded on the floor as he left the room, taking the last of the chaos with him.

She didn't watch him go, unable to tear her eyes away from the man who held her heart.

"What? You didn't think I would declare my love and just leave it at that, did you?"

"Well, no. But I figured you'd at least wait until you're out of the hospital before we took things further."

He shrugged, then grimaced as the movement shifted his incision. "No use half-assing things." His fingers walked over the blanket to curl around hers. "I love you, Macy. Now that my brain's caught up to my heart, there's no denying it, nor do I want to. I just want to be with you. Always. Marry me?"

Tears swam in her vision, and she sniffed. "I should have recorded this, so I can play it back for you once you're no longer high on painkillers and denying it all."

His smile grew. "It's not the drugs talking. Marry me. Spend the rest of your life calling me on my bullshit."

Heart swelling so much it hurt, she rose far enough from her chair to lean over him, her face only inches from his. "On one condition."

"What's that?"

"We don't go camping for our honeymoon. No wilderness of any kind."

He chuckled, then immediately groaned. "God, that hurt." He drew in a slow breath. "But yes, no camping."

She grinned. "Good." Her smile faded as she stared down at him. His dark gaze glittered in the overhead lights. "I love you, Brady. So much. I would be honored to be your wife."

That beautiful smile of his blossomed over his handsome face, taking some of the pain and fatigue with it. "It's me who's honored. I'm a damn fool, but I'm so glad you gave me another chance. I promise not to waste it."

"I won't let you." She closed the gap between them, sealing the promise with a kiss.

EPILOGUE

The thunder of hundreds of hooves on the hard-packed earth rang through Brady's chest as he rode alongside the herd atop Titan. It felt good to be back in the saddle. Ahead, one of the hands opened the gate to let the cattle into the pen nearest the barns. Brady whistled as he drove the animals through the opening. He stopped beside his dad as he closed the gate.

"How are you feeling, son?"

"Fine."

"No aches?"

"Nothing I wasn't expecting." His hips and knees would protest today's long ride later, but his chest felt fine.

"Good." Lee pointed toward the opposite side of the corral. "Someone's waiting on you."

He turned to see Macy standing on the fence rail, her auburn hair blowing in the wind. A grin bloomed on his face. "I'll see you later, Dad."

Lee smirked. "Not too much. We still have work to do."

Brady tossed a smile at him as he rode away, rounding the perimeter of the fence. As he got closer, he noticed Dan and

Denise standing with her, along with Hannah and Jessie, and one surprise visitor—Asa Mitchell. He pulled up next to them and dismounted.

"Brady!" Jessie launched herself at him, wrapping him in a hug.

He laughed and looped Titan's reins around the fence rail before picking her up. "Hey there, munchkin."

"Guess what?"

"What?"

"Dan took us to an awesome museum in Colorado Springs. It had a real brain on display. And dinosaur bones!"

"It did?"

"Yep!"

"The brain was gross, but the dinosaurs were cool," Hannah said.

"Well, I'm glad you guys had fun." He set Jessie on her feet, then looked at Dan and Denise. "You been back long?"

Dan shook his head. "A few minutes. We drove in and Hannah saw Mr. Mitchell talking to Macy." He grinned at the girl. "She begged us to stop."

Hannah's cheeks reddened. "I'm a fan. Sue me."

Asa laughed. "Never, darlin'. I'm glad you stopped to say hello."

She blushed harder.

Denise wrapped an arm around her daughter's shoulders. "Come on. Let's get home and cool off. I don't know about the rest of you, but I'm hot and could use a glass of iced tea."

"Can I have lemonade?" Jessie bounced up and down on the balls of her feet.

"Of course."

"Yay!" She took off for the car. "Bye, Macy! Bye, Brady! Bye, Mr. Asa!" she yelled over her shoulder.

"I guess we're going," Dan said, an amused smile on his face. He shook his head and started after her.

Denise and Hannah waved and followed him.

Brady chuckled as he watched them leave, then held out a hand to Asa. "Asa, it's good to see you. What brings you here?" They shook hands, then Brady stepped back to wrap an arm around Macy's waist after she hopped off the fence to stand next to him.

"I came to look at a filly Knox has, then decided to stop by and see you and your new bride. I was just giving Macy my congratulations before her sisters stopped by to say hello."

Brady smiled. "Thanks. Sorry we didn't send you an invite. It was spur of the moment." After he left the hospital, neither of them wanted to wait to start the next chapter of their lives. Tomorrow wasn't promised, and they wanted to take advantage of every minute they were given together.

Asa waved a hand and smiled. "It's fine. I wouldn't have been able to make it, anyway. I was on tour."

"You're retired now, though, right?"

"Yeah. I hung up my guitar and traded it for some shit-kickers and bowed legs."

Brady laughed. "How's it going being a full-time rancher?"

"The ranching part's not so bad. I like being out in the field." He shrugged, frowning. "Gets me away from the chaos at home."

"Chaos? What chaos?" Macy asked. "Don't you live with your dad?"

"Yep. And our brand-new housekeeper, Daisy."

Brady shared an amused look with Macy at the exasperation in his voice. "What's wrong with her?"

Asa rolled his eyes. "A lot of things. Mostly, she likes to annoy me at every turn."

"Maybe you just need to spend some time with her," Macy suggested. "You know, get to know her."

"No. I need to spend less time with her. With any woman, honestly. No offense."

"What's wrong with us?" She propped her free hand on her hip.

"With you, nothing. You're great. But most others?" He shook his head. "They want one of two things from me: sex or money. Sometimes both."

"What does Daisy want?" Brady asked. He found it hard to believe Silas would employ someone who was after either of those things from his son.

A perplexed frown drew his eyebrows down. "I don't know. I can't figure her out."

Macy giggled.

Asa turned his bright blue eyes on her. "What?"

"Do yourself a favor and get to know her. I bet you'll be surprised."

"What makes you so sure of that? She's always contradicting me and refusing to do what I ask. But she has no problem doing what my dad asks of her."

"Have you tried asking instead of demanding?"

"I don't—"

She waved him off with a laugh. "Of course you do. Asa, do you want to know why I never said yes to you?"

"You mean other than because you were hung up on this son of a bitch?" He motioned to Brady.

She rolled her eyes. "Yes, other than that."

"Sure. Hit me."

"You're too sure of yourself."

"That's a bad thing?"

"Sometimes. I didn't want to be just another piece of arm candy. You're used to getting your way. People bend over backward to make you happy, including the women you date. I would never be happy in a relationship where I'm always deferring to my partner."

Brady snorted. "That's the truth. She can never just agree with me."

Macy patted his arm. "It's okay, babe. Not all of us can be right all the time."

Asa laughed, then shook his head. "I envy you two. And all your friends and siblings. You've found something that I don't think is in the cards for me. Not that I ever really wanted that sort of thing. But if I did, I doubt it would ever happen. My life—my notoriety—just isn't conducive to that kind of relationship."

"Maybe. Or maybe it's closer than you think."

He frowned. "You mean Daisy?"

She nodded.

He scoffed. "No."

Macy lifted one shoulder and looked up at Brady. "Don't knock it until you really get to know her. She might surprise you."

"She's right," Brady said, smiling down at his wife. "The best thing that could ever happen to you might be right in front of your face."

Asa groaned. "God, marriage made you sappy." He waved a hand. "I'm going back to Knox's. He and I can celebrate our bachelorhood."

Brady laughed. "You do that. Invite us to the wedding."

Asa glanced back, a grin quirking one corner of his mouth. He shook his head. "You all are dreaming."

Macy giggled and waved. "Bye, Asa. Tell your father we said hello."

His smile turned genuine. "I will. It was good to see you both."

"You, too." Brady lifted a hand and watched the other man walk toward a shiny gray truck parked in front of the barn.

"Should we take bets on how long until he marries her?" Macy asked.

"Nah. Asa's just mysterious enough it could be a few weeks or a few months. Hell, it could be even longer."

"True. But I don't think it will take long."

He looked down at her. "No?"

"No. Watching his friends fall in love has got him thinking. And this Daisy sounds like she might be the woman to change his mind."

"You haven't even met her."

"I don't need to. His tone and the look in his eyes tell me everything I need to know."

"Is that right?" A corner of his mouth lifted. He leaned down.

She nodded, giving him a soft smile. "Yep."

"Well, I'm just glad you weren't the one to do that for him." He dipped his head closer.

"There was never a danger of that. You're the only one I ever wanted."

A smile curved his mouth. "Good." He closed the gap to settle a sweet kiss on her lips.

∾

Keep reading for a sneak peek at Asa's story, *Sweetness*, book 1 in the *Pine Ridge* series.

Thank you for reading Scorched! I hope you enjoyed it.

Want to read an EXCLUSIVE and FREE book? Sign up for my mailing list. You can find the sign-up form on my website, ashleyaquinn.com. My list also receives sneak peeks of my latest work and access to exclusive giveaways. Also, please consider leaving a rating or review on Amazon and or Goodreads. It would be greatly appreciated!

Thanks again for reading!
- Ashley

~

Keep reading for a sneak peek at Book 6, Light of Dawn in the Broken Bow Series.

SWEETNESS

PINE RIDGE
BOOK 1

PROLOGUE

Bones aching, Silas Mitchell dragged himself into his bedroom to take a shower and crash. He was getting too old to wrangle cattle like he was in his thirties. Crossing to the dresser, he opened his underwear drawer. His shoulders drooped as he stared down in defeat. He was out of clean skivvies.

His gaze wandered to the heap of laundry in the corner. Dammit. Sighing, he tipped his head back, looking up at the ceiling, exasperated.

He slammed the drawer shut and stomped over to the pile, scooping it up.

"Frickin' salesman, stealing my damned housekeeper away," he muttered, descending the stairs. "I don't have time for all this shit." He entered the laundry room and threw his armload of clothes into the washer. Dumping detergent in the dispenser, he slammed the lid and spun the dial, then punched the button to turn it on.

That task done, he stormed down to the kitchen and grabbed the newspaper off the counter and opened it to the classifieds, looking for a number to call to place an ad. He'd do it first thing in the morning. He leafed through it, but all he saw was a web address.

Everything has to be online nowadays. He sighed and pulled out his phone, scrolling through his contacts until he found the number for his foreman, Chet Red Feather. He pressed send.

Chet picked up on the second ring. "Hi, Silas. What's up?"

"Sorry to bother you. I know we just finished up, and you were looking forward to a bit of family time, but I need a hand with something."

"Oh? What's wrong?"

"I need a woman."

There was a pause. The only sound was Chet's baby, Sloan, squalling in the background.

"I'm sorry, what?"

"A woman. Or a man. I'm not picky. I just need a damn housekeeper. I'm tired of running out of clean skivvies."

Chet laughed. "That's much better than what was running through my mind. Okay. So why are you calling me?"

"I want to put an ad in the newspaper, but it's all online. I don't know how to do that crap. Asa's not here to do it, so can you or Marci come help me?"

"Actually, I can do it here. Hang on a second." Silas heard Chet move through his house, the sound of the baby crying getting louder, then quieter as he moved.

"You want it in the Billings paper?"

"Yep."

Chet paused as he typed, the click-clack of the keyboard coming over the line. "Okay. I have your information entered. What do you want the ad to say?"

"That I want a housekeeper. Someone to clean, maybe do some light cooking. Room and board included."

There was another pause.

"Okay if I use the ranch credit card? Since this is a ranch expense?"

"Yep."

More clicking filled the silence.

"All right, it's in. Any applicants are supposed to send a resume to the ranch email."

Silas breathed a sigh of relief. With any luck, he'd have someone new out here soon to take over Jeannie's duties. "Thanks, Chet. I appreciate it."

"Not a problem. I'll see you tomorrow."

"Yep. Kiss that baby for me."

"Will do."

Silas hung up. His eyes landed on the dishes in the sink. *Jesus.* It's a wonder there weren't flies swarming the house. Rolling up his sleeves, he turned on the water.

ONE

Daisy O'Malley stared at herself in the mirror, fiddling with the ends of her thick auburn hair. Her high-neck, crushed velvet black dress looked like something she'd have worn at one of her high school choir concerts back in the day. God, she looked so dumpy! It was no wonder she was still single.

She scoffed and rolled her eyes. *Yeah, that's why.* It had nothing to do with her six overbearing brothers, who thought it was their job to hand-pick her husband. Case in point, it was Valentine's Day, and she had a blind date. Someone her brother, Kyle, worked with at his software firm. Ethan Byrnes. Kyle swore he was a nice Irish Catholic who did *not* live with his mother still.

She sighed and stepped away from the mirror, stuffing her feet into a pair of black boots. The doorbell rang as she picked up her black clutch. Her cat, Tallulah, jumped up on the back of the couch and meowed as she passed, wanting scratched. Daisy ran a hand over her soft gray and white fur, then continued to the door.

Slipping the security chain off, she flipped open the deadbolts and grasped the knob. She inhaled a deep breath to shore up her confidence and opened the door.

Her eyes went wide as she took in the man on her doorstep. He looked like a bulldog! Stocky and short—so short!—he smiled at her, deep lines bracketing his brown eyes. His light brown hair was combed straight back to within an inch of its life and shellacked into place. The light from the hallway bounced off of it, making it look wet. A light gray suit strained at the seams over his muscular frame. Dark chest hair peeked over the top of the black t-shirt he wore with the suit.

"Wow, you're even prettier than the picture Kyle showed me." He raked his eyes over her, lingering on her chest.

"Thank you. You're... different too." Before she agreed to this date, she made Kyle show her a picture. The last time she went out with one of the men her brothers picked, she'd spent two hours in the company of a man who devoted way too much time to his spray tan. Ethan looked normal in the head-shot Kyle showed her. Now she knew why it was his security badge photo she'd seen and not some candid shot.

"Yeah, my hair's grown since I had that picture taken," he said with a smile.

"Mmm, that must be it."

"Are you ready to go?"

She nodded. "I just need to put my coat on." She stepped back to open the hall closet and take out her long wool pea coat. Putting it on, she walked into the hall and locked her door.

"So, where are we going?" she asked as they made their way to the elevator.

"Kyle said you like Italian food, so I booked us a table at Giancarlo's Bistro. I hope that's okay."

"I've never heard of it, but I'm sure it'll be fine," she said, stepping onto the elevator.

"Oh, it's great. It belongs to a friend of mine from school. It's his family's place."

Which meant he wanted them to see him with her. Whether it was to show off or for their approval, she wasn't sure. Maybe both.

The elevator doors dinged, and they stepped off, walking through the lobby of her building to the street. He hailed a cab, and they were soon winding their way through the streets of Chicago to the restaurant.

The drive was short, and the cab pulled up to a building ten blocks away. Daisy got out and glanced around as she waited for Ethan to join her. The area wasn't the greatest, but it also wasn't the worst, and the restaurant looked welcoming.

Ethan held the door for her, and she stepped inside. The heavenly smell of pasta sauce and garlic bread enveloped her. She really did love Italian food.

"Hi, Ethan. Mama said you were bringing a date here tonight." The young woman at the host stand smiled at them.

"Hi Meghan. This is Daisy. Daisy, meet Meghan Turati."

Daisy smiled and offered her a wave. "It's nice to meet you."

Meghan smiled back and picked up a couple of menus. "You too. Follow me, and I'll get you seated."

They wound through the tables to a spot near the back. Ethan pulled out her chair for her, then took his place across the table. Daisy shrugged out of her coat and took the menu Meghan offered.

"What can I get you guys to drink?" Meghan asked.

"I'll take a glass of that nice cab you guys got in. Daisy will have water."

Daisy's brow slammed down. She already knew this date wouldn't end well. "Actually, I'll take a glass of pinot grigio, please."

Meghan raised a brow, her eyes darting to Ethan before

going back to her. She nodded. "Your server is George. He'll be right over with those."

"Thank you," Daisy said.

Ethan fidgeted in his seat, watching Meghan for a moment as she walked away before turning to her, frowning. "You drink?"

She stared at him for a second, then nodded. "I'm not a drunk, but I like a glass of wine now and then, yes."

"Hmm... Kyle said you didn't."

One corner of her mouth lifted. "Kyle would like to think I don't, because he wants me to stay his baby sister. But I'm twenty-eight and can enjoy an alcoholic beverage just like any other adult."

He pressed his lips into a thin smile and nodded.

This was going so well... She opened her menu and rolled her eyes behind it, wondering what else her brother told him. Ethan was no doubt under the impression she was some goodie-goodie who was content to let her man make all her decisions. Truth be told, she couldn't fault her brothers for thinking that. She let them make most of her decisions. But it was really beginning to wear thin.

Their server walked up with their drinks and asked for their orders. She asked for the lasagna while Ethan went with the chicken parmesan. The young man took their menus and disappeared.

Daisy folded her hands in her lap to keep from fidgeting with the silverware. She hated first dates. They were always so awkward.

"So, Kyle said you're a baker."

She nodded. "I work for the place a couple blocks from my apartment. Sugar and Spice."

He hummed. "Never been there."

"You should try it. It's great."

He smiled. "You'll have to bring me some treats on our next date. I'd love to see what you can do."

She gave him a polite smile. Unless the tempo of this date picked up, there wouldn't be a second one. "Tell me, Ethan, what do you like to do for fun?"

"Fun?"

"Yes, fun."

His brow furrowed as he thought. "I box some."

That explained his stocky build.

"What else?"

"Um, I like video games. I just bought a new console, so I've been playing on it a lot lately."

She swallowed a groan. He was a man-child! "That's nice. Do you like to spend time outdoors?" She loved going to the city parks and walking. When she had time, she drove out of the city to some nature trails in the suburbs.

He shook his head. "Not really. I have terrible allergies, so the only time of year I can be outside without being miserable are the winter months, and it's just too cold."

Daisy loved winter. The cold was exhilarating. She bundled up in her parka and mittens and walked the trails just like she would in the summer.

"What about you?" he asked. "What do you do for fun?"

"I hike."

"Oh."

She picked up her wineglass and took a sip, wondering why she kept agreeing to these dates. Ethan seemed nice, but they had little in common. Just like every other man she dated at her brothers' request.

Taking another sip, she set the glass down and did her best to listen as Ethan started talking about his new video game. She was going to kill Kyle later.

The server brought their food, and Daisy dug in, happy to

have an excuse not to talk. That didn't stop Ethan, though. He stuffed a bite of his entrée in his mouth and chewed away while he continued to regale her with stories of his prowess on his latest gaming obsession. Partially masticated chicken wallowed around in his mouth while he did so. It was nauseating. She did her best to keep her eyes on her own plate as she poked at her lasagna, only looking up enough to make it look like she was listening.

"Something wrong with your food?"

Daisy glanced up from her plate at his question. Her lasagna was delicious, but watching him eat and talk killed her appetite. "Oh, no. It's fine. I'm just not very hungry, I guess."

"You better eat. Mama Turati will be upset if you don't eat."

She shrugged. "I'm not going to force myself to eat if I'm not hungry. I'll make sure she knows it wasn't her cooking."

He frowned. "I guess that would be okay. We'll tell her you're on a diet and filled up on water so you wouldn't eat as much. She'd believe that."

Daisy's eyebrows slammed down. "How about we just tell her I'm not hungry?" Because she most certainly was not on a diet.

His expression turned thoughtful. Daisy's eyes widened. How could he not read the hostility in her voice and on her face?

"I think it's better if we tell her you're on a diet. A woman like you, she wouldn't believe you weren't hungry."

"A woman like me? What does that mean?"

"Well, you know." He gestured to her torso. "You're... voluptuous."

"Voluptuous." She set her fork down carefully and folded her hands in her lap.

"Yes. Very. And don't get me wrong, I'm a fan." His eyes landed on her chest and stayed there. "But you have a few pounds to spare."

Humiliation turned Daisy's cheeks bright red. The chair legs scraped the tile floor as she pushed away from the table and stood. "I'm sorry, but this isn't going to work out." She picked up her coat and put it on.

"Where are you going? We haven't finished eating. And there's cannoli for dessert."

She paused buttoning up her coat to stare down at him, incredulous. "Really? You sure my fat ass can handle it?" Shaking her head, she picked up her purse and walked away.

The sound of his chair moving across the floor and his footsteps hurrying after her made her sigh. She just wanted to go home.

"Wait! You can't leave." He ran around to stand in front of her.

She arched a brow. "Why not? You've insulted me, stared at my breasts through most of our date, and frankly, are a disgusting eater. I've had quite enough."

His face turned red, and veins popped out on his forehead and in his neck. "Your brother won't be happy about this."

She shrugged. "That's his problem. Goodnight." She walked around him and hurried out the door before he could follow her.

Her heels clacked on the sidewalk as she strode down the block toward her apartment. A chill permeated the air, but she didn't feel it. She was too angry. The nerve of that man! So she indulged in a pastry or two at work on occasion. Whoop-dee-doo. He was nothing to write home about when he barely came to her shoulders. She couldn't believe Kyle thought that —that pig!—was an acceptable suitor. Her brothers had set her up with some doozies over the years, but Ethan Byrnes might take the cake. None of the other men ever dared insinuate she was fat.

Still fuming fifteen minutes later, she let herself into her apartment. Tallulah ran up and chirped.

"Yes, I know I'm back sooner than expected. Mr. Byrnes is an asshole."

The cat laid down and rolled onto her back, feet in the air. Daisy smiled and bent down to scratch her between her front feet. "Who needs a man when I have you?" She certainly didn't need that particular man.

Rising, she put her coat away. As she shut the closet door, her cellphone rang. She groaned. It was probably Kyle. No doubt Ethan called him to complain.

She took the phone from her purse and looked at the screen. Kyle's face stared back at her. She contemplated not answering, but knew he would just keep calling, eventually showing up at her apartment if she didn't answer.

Daisy slid her thumb over the screen. "Hello?"

"Why did you leave your date early?"

She sank onto the couch. Tallulah jumped into her lap and she stroked the cat's silky fur. "You tell me. What did Ethan tell you?"

"He said you threw a hissy fit about the food, then left."

She rolled her eyes. "I did not throw a fit about the food. The food was fantastic. I just wasn't able to eat it because he insisted on talking around a mouthful of half-chewed chicken parmesan. When I told him I wasn't hungry, he told me that Mama Turati would be upset that I didn't eat. I said we'd just tell her I didn't have much of an appetite. He said we should tell her I was on a diet and filled up on water first so I wouldn't eat much. I argued what I suggested was fine, but he insisted we use his excuse, then told me it was more believable because I could stand to lose a few pounds."

A short silence met her explanation. "Oh."

"Yeah. What could you have possibly seen in that man that made you think he'd be a suitable match for me? I mean, seriously, Kyle. What the hell?"

"Don't curse at me. He's a hard worker and has always

been nice to me."

"You're a man."

Kyle sighed. "Maybe he's just old-fashioned. You should give him another chance."

"When cakes fly!"

"Come on, Dais. He comes from a good Catholic family. Mom and Dad would love that."

That might be so, but she could guarantee her mother would string the man up by his ankles after hearing Daisy's story tonight.

"Well, regardless of what they'd think, I don't see another date with him in my future. Thanks for trying. I'm going to make myself a snack now and go to bed. Gotta get up for work."

"Daisy—"

"Have a good night. Love you. Bye." She hung up before he could say more, then turned off her ringer.

With a sigh, she laid her head back against the cushions. She was so tired of dealing with her brothers. They drove her crazy with their overprotective, domineering attitudes. She loved them, but being treated like a teenager still at the age of twenty-eight was growing increasingly tiresome. It was time to take back some control of her life.

She looked down at Tallulah, her eyes straying to the crushed velvet dress she wore.

Ugh. That control was going to start with her wardrobe. Tomorrow, she vowed, she would go shopping for some different clothes. Nothing too crazy, but she'd like to get something that didn't look like a funeral dress from the eighteen-hundreds.

"Come on, Lulabell." She stood up, holding the cat. "Let's find a snack and hit the hay. I'm tired."

Tallulah let out a short meow, purring as Daisy carried her toward the kitchen and the ice cream waiting in the freezer.

About the Author

Ashley started writing in her teens and never stopped. Her first novel, Smoky Mountain Murder, came out in 2016, and she has since published two more series and has plans for more. When not writing, you can find her with her nose stuck in a book or watching some terrible disaster movie on SyFy. An avid baseball fan, she also enjoys crafting and cooking. She lives in Ohio with her husband, two kids, three cats, and one very wild shepherd mix.

Website: https://ashleyaquinn.com

goodreads.com/ashleyaquinn

amazon.com/Ashley-A-Quinn/e/B07HCT4QST